## Elaine spun round with a little cry, clutching the rug around her tightly

Kemp was standing in the doorway, a storm lantern in his hand, his shirt soaked and clinging to his body.

"Why did you move my gown?" she asked breathlessly. "You have no right..."

"I had every right." He took a step nearer her. "I have thrown a lot more overboard, Elaine. I threw your lands and title, your inheritance, your wealth and your wedding ring." His eyes gleamed as she held up her hand, bare of its gold band. "From now on you are a pirate's woman!"

KATE BUCHAN was born in Nottingham and educated in Hertfordshire and at Edinburgh University, where she read history. She then worked for various publishers before becoming a free-lance editor. During this period she began writing short stories and articles, and in due course she gave up editing to write full time.

*Buccaneer Bride*, her fifth historical novel, was written while living—with her husband, two sons and seven cats—in a rambling, pink-washed Tudor farmhouse not far from the lovely old town of Woodbridge and the beautiful Suffolk marshes, which are the setting for this story.

# HARLEQUIN HISTORICAL

# KATE BUCHAN
## *Buccaneer Bride*

## *Harlequin Books*

TORONTO • NEW YORK • LONDON
AMSTERDAM • PARIS • SYDNEY • HAMBURG
STOCKHOLM • ATHENS • TOKYO • MILAN

Harlequin Historical edition published January 1987
ISBN 0-373-30211-8

Original hardcover edition published in 1986
by Mills & Boon Limited

# PROLOGUE

THE TIDE had turned. Already little eddies of mud were appearing at the edge of the salt grass and the wind was veering. Elaine Howard felt it on her cheek as she stood, swathed in a dark cloak, at the river's edge watching the ship drop her lines and begin to ease her way out into the main current of the deserted river. It would soon be nightfall.

On deck Elaine could see the silent men standing by the ratlines and clinging high in the rigging as the dark sails dropped soundlessly from the yardarms and bellied before the wind, giving the vessel steerage on the tide. No pennant or flag flew from the raked masts, and no name showed on the blackened planking of her hull.

A lone figure stood erect on the quarterdeck, his face like carved stone as he turned his ship down-river towards the sea. Elaine ran a few steps along the bank, her shoes slipping on the grass, still straining her eyes for Tom, but even now there was no sign of him, and she blinked back her tears, her gaze drawn inexorably to that single figure. Tall and broad-shouldered, he radiated sinister power, his eyes coolly surveying the darkening river ahead. Abruptly his gaze shifted towards the shore and for an instant she felt it rest on her. Then he turned his head away as the ship moved silently off into the dark.

In the shadow of the trees, a second figure had been watching the vessel leave. As he stepped forward, impatiently parting the fronds of willow to see better, he stopped, catching sight of Elaine for the first time. At once he drew back so that she should not notice him, and studied her. At that distance he could see nothing but the dark green cloak, the soft hood pulled well up over her hair and held fast with one hand as she raised the other to her eyes, trying to focus on the dark shape as it vanished into the night. Only the slap of water against the ship's prow as she gathered speed betrayed her presence in the distance.

He moved forward stealthily, his soft leather boots making no sound on the dew-wet grass, his hand on the hilt of his sword as he stopped about five feet from her. The cloak still concealed everything about her save her stature, which was slight.

'Mistress! A word with you, if you please!' His voice was harsh in the silence.

Elaine spun round. He had an impression of huge amber-coloured eyes in a small oval face and long silken hair the shade of ripe wheat as her hood slipped back. The slim figure wore a servant's plain dress and apron, and he had a swift impression of skin as fine and pale as that on any woman he had ever seen. Momentarily stunned by this unexpected vision of beauty, he did not move. And in that second she whirled out of his reach and fled up the bank.

As he gathered his wits and turned to follow her, the sound of a horse's hooves echoed over the dry ground. He glimpsed a fleeting shadow as a horse leapt away through the trees, and she was gone.

He did not bother to chase her. He would never catch her now; his own horse was liveried at an inn in Woodbridge and he had left it when he strolled down the River Deben from the bustling quays and boatyards, curious to follow up the rumour about the ship anchored below Kingston Point.

Sir Edward Brandon, pirate-catcher to his grace King Henry VIII, turned back thoughtfully to where the vessel had slipped out of sight. If, as he suspected, this was the pirate ship, maybe that young woman had a friend or a lover on board. He smiled softly to himself. It would not be hard to find her again in Woodbridge; hers was a face he would not forget, and once he had her, his job would be easy. It only took one lead, one member of the crew or their family to betray the others. And it was a very exceptional man—or woman—who could resist the methods of persuasion available to him in the dungeons of the King's castles as he travelled round the coasts of England.

He smiled as he began to walk thoughtfully back towards the lights of Woodbridge. Tomorrow he would introduce himself to the rich merchants who had begged the King for help and begin to buy in supplies of wool, cloth and grain, spices and rich silks and wines for the royal storehouses— the reason he always gave to explain his presence in the ports of the realm. Tomorrow his hunt for the pirates who haunted this particular shore would begin. But this time his quest would be a little different from the usual, for it was on his own doorstep, in Suffolk, and in addition to the duty he performed for the King was another—far more pleasurable—for himself. Tomorrow he would meet the woman who had topped his list of possible brides; the daughter of one of the richest merchants in Suffolk; the woman he had chosen to be his wife.

# CHAPTER
## ONE

ELAINE HAD been woken that late May morning by the rattle of wooden rings as the heavy tapestry curtains were thrown back and the clear dawn light flooded into the room. For a moment she lay still beneath the embroidered tester, still dazed with sleep, then she sat up abruptly, clutching the bedclothes to her near-naked shoulders as she saw a figure standing at the window, pushing back the shutters.

'Tom? Is that you? What are you doing here?'

'Sssh!' At the sound of her voice, her brother turned and put his finger to his lips, conscious of her maid asleep in the ante-room. He left the window and came to perch on the edge of her bed.

'I had to talk to you, Elaine. Listen, sweetheart! I want you to do something for me.' Tom's handsome face was unusually troubled as he looked at his sister propped against the feather pillows, her ash-blonde hair spilt in tangled curls across the sheets.

'What is it? You sound so solemn!' Staring at him, she felt a sudden tremor of fear, thinking automatically of the person dearest to them both. 'Is it something to do with Father?'

He shook his head with a rueful smile. 'Not unless Papa has taken to breaking the King's peace in his old age.' He raised his hand to stop her speaking. 'No, I'm the felon in the family, I'm afraid, and I need your help.' He paused as she stared at him, puzzled by his words. 'I never wanted to tell you all this, sweetheart,' he went on, 'but I think I must.' He frowned, picking at the silk counterpane on her bed. 'Just in case something happens to me, someone here ought to know the truth of where I am, and you are the only person I can tell.'

Her fear deepened as she watched her brother's anxiety,

9

and pulling her shawl from the bedpost where she had thrown it the night before, she drew it round her shoulders and half knelt up beneath the bedclothes like a child, reaching out her hand to his in her uncertainty.

He gave a tight smile. 'Did you ever hear of the raid on *Santa Maria*?'

'Cousin Richard's ship? Of course I heard. She was attacked by pirates in the North Sea, and he lost everything. I remember him coming to tell Papa about it. He was so angry that I thought he would have apoplexy . . .' Her voice tailed away as she studied her brother's face. 'Why do you ask?'

'I was on the ship which carried out that raid, Elaine. In fact she is half mine. It was I who planned where to strike, and when.'

Elaine went white. 'No, I don't believe you. Dear God, Tom, men died on that ship! Tell me it isn't true!' She slumped back on her heels as she studied her brother's face.

'I'm afraid it is true, sweetheart.' His strong hands gripped hers suddenly. 'I wouldn't have had you find out for worlds, but there are reasons you must know. No, you must listen to me!' His hold on her hand began to hurt as she tried to pull free. 'I go on another raid this evening. It may take me away for longer than I intended, so there are two services you must perform for me.'

'No, Tom!' Elaine dragged her hands free at last and threw herself from the bed. 'I won't listen! I don't want to hear any more. If what you say is true, then it's despicable! How could you betray your own family! Oh, Tom, why? And who else? Have you done it to our friends? For all I know, you have robbed Papa's own ships!' As the full horror of his admission sank in, she began to shake uncontrollably. That her beloved brother, whom she had adored all her life, should admit so calmly to being no more than a brutal pirate and a murderer filled her with terror and loathing. It was as if in the space of a few short minutes he had become a stranger to her.

'Elaine, listen . . .

'No!' She raised her hands to her ears and tried to shut

out the sound of his voice. 'No, Tom. Please! Just go away!'

He had followed her across the room. 'Sweet Elaine! Please just try and understand a little. You want to know why I did it? I'll tell you. For excitement; for danger; to relieve these fat, rich men of a small part of their wealth, and with it to buy freedom! Freedom to feel the ship beneath my feet! To travel; to learn to steer by the stars and to ride the wind! To be my own master, not my father's lackey.' He shook her gently. 'Do you know where my future lies? It lies in that counting-house and in the ware-house down by the Deben, collecting money while other men have the adventure. I have begged Papa a thousand times to let me go with the ships to learn my trade, but no, never! "Why go?" he says. "Stay here, Tom, and learn the business end; I need you with me, Tom. One day it will all be yours, Tom." One day! But even while I am at his side learning the trade, I can see he still thinks of me as a child in short coats. Well, on *Black Witch* I am the master, and I make men like my father jump through hoops at my command!'

Elaine looked at him, frozen with horror, seeing for the first time the reckless colour in his cheeks and the wildness in his eyes.

'You sound as if you hate Papa!' she whispered.

Tom shook his head slowly. 'No, that's the strange part. I don't hate him. I would never hurt him if I could help it; you must never think that, Elaine. It is his way of life I hate, and what he has come to stand for.'

'Supposing you are caught?' Her lips had gone dry.

He grinned. 'I won't be.' He saw the softening of her expression, and stooped and kissed her gently on the fore-head. 'I knew you'd understand,' he said softly.

'No, Tom!' She shook her head violently. 'It means that men have died at your hand.' She shuddered. 'You cannot justify murder—and robbery—just . . .' she hesitated, fumbling over the words in her anguish, 'just for excitement and adventure! Oh, Tom, for pity's sake stop it now. Don't go, I beg you.' She clutched at his arms.

'I have to, sweetheart.' He removed her hands gently. 'I'm too much involved. It's my plan; she's half my ship;

my partner needs me and I don't intend to let him down. Now, are you going to help me?'

'Help you?' Elaine stared at him in real horror. 'No, I won't help you! Never! You disgust me!' Tears filled her eyes. 'What would Mama have said if she had known?'

'Mama is long since dead, Elaine,' Tom said harshly. 'And all I am asking is for you to pass a packet of letters to a friend of mine; not so great a burden, surely? It will not involve setting foot outside this house, I assure you, so your pretty conscience will not be in danger.' He tightened his lips with a stubbornness she recognised well.

'And if I refuse?' The set of her own chin matched his as she angrily blinked away the tears.

'You won't refuse.' He reached into his doublet and produced the packet, which he threw down on the bed. 'Her name is Jane Lockesley. Keep them safe, under lock and key. The chances are I shall return before she comes to claim them, but in case anything happens'—a shadow crossed his face for a moment—'I want to be sure she gets them.' He smiled at her pleadingly. 'Please do this for me.'

Elaine stared at him, the anger in her eyes mixed with fear. 'Don't go, Tom. Stay and give them to her yourself. *Please!*'

'I can't, Elaine.'

'You mean you want to go,' she burst out. 'You want to be in danger! You don't care about us! You're being irresponsible and stupid and stubborn! Think about Papa. If he found out, it would kill him. You know it would!'

Tom frowned. 'He must never find out, Elaine. Perhaps I am being irresponsible—all the things you say, but that's the way I am.' He shrugged. 'And, anyway, I'm going on only two more trips, and then I'll sell out my share of *Black Witch* to Guy and come home and be a dutiful son. Does that please you?'

She shook her head. 'Why two more trips, Tom? Why?'

'Because these particular schemes are mine; without my information, we wouldn't be able to go for such big prizes.'

She gasped. 'You mean you use knowledge from Papa; information he's trusted you with?'

'Of course I do. I'm perfectly placed here. I hear everything, not only from Papa and his colleagues, but his rivals too.'

Elaine was white with anger. 'I think you're despicable. I hope you're caught!'

Tom grinned. 'Thank you, sister dear. I'd best be on my way, then. *Witch* lies at Kingston Point. We sail on tonight's tide.' He strode to the door, and paused. 'Just in case you need to find me, the landlord at the King's Head usually knows Guy Kemp's plans.'

'I won't need to find you, Tom!' She turned away from him, trying to hold back her tears.

'And you won't at least wish me God speed?'

'God would not bless a trip such as yours,' she whispered in anguish.

Her brother made no reply. She heard the door open and close softly.

It was too late to call him back, even if she had wanted to; too late to unsay her angry words. With tears in her eyes she ran to the window, watching as Tom let himself out of the small door in the wall below. He strode quickly out of sight without looking back.

Bitterly she turned to the packet he had left lying on her bed. Picking it up, she turned it over in her hands. The back of the vellum was sealed; the front bore only the simple inscription: 'To: Mistress Jane Lockesley.' For a moment she was tempted to break it open and see what was so important that she had had to be let into Tom's secrets to ensure its safe delivery; more than a love letter, surely? Then, suddenly, she was afraid. Whatever it was, she did not want to know. She dropped the packet into the small jewel chest on the table by her bed and locked it, then she hid the tiny key in the knot-hole of one of the beams of her bedroom ceiling. 'Oh, Tom,' she whispered, 'please come back safely. Please!'

For a long time after Tom had gone, she stood at the stone mullioned window of her room, watching the sun rise above the yew hedges which surrounded the ornamental gardens of King's Brook Manor, and slowly, as she calmed, she began to think about what Tom had told her. She could never condone what he had done, but perhaps she could understand. It was, after all, the same rebellion she had tried so hard to hide in herself; the same resentment against their father's obsession with business. Because Tom was a man, he had been able to act, while all she had managed to do was to refuse the succession of rich, stout, merchants' sons who had been paraded before her as potential husbands, until her exasperated father claimed that she seemed determined to die an old maid.

She sighed deeply. Even if Tom had admitted that he was engaged in piracy, she still loved him—nothing could change that—and her grief was touched with terrible fear as she thought of the danger he must have faced in the past and which he must face again, and soon.

The day passed in a miserable dream as she went about her chores, supervising the huge household, and working in the still-room and the herb gardens, and by evening she knew that she had to go to Kingston Point to see Tom before his ship sailed. She had to tell him that she did wish him well. She could not let him leave thinking she did not care.

Climbing the stairs to her room, she sent for her maid. 'Mab, do you know when the tide is high at the town quay?' She was sitting at her carved oak writing-table, a quill in her hand, a memorandum open before her.

Mab was a plump, dark-haired girl with a happy wide mouth which displayed a gap between her two front teeth. 'Why, mistress, you're never working for your father?' Automatically the girl bent to pick up a fallen shift. 'I heard it was three hours before midnight or thereabouts. But the *Bonaventure* doesn't sail for days yet . . .'

'I know that!' *Bonaventure* was her father's flagship. Impatiently Elaine stood up and threw down her pen, abandoning all pretence of writing. 'I want to borrow one of your gowns, Mab.'

'You want to . . .' The girl gaped at her, her hands on her ample hips. 'Now why on earth should you do that, mistress, with all your lovely things?'

Elaine sighed. 'Use your head, Mab. Because I don't want to be seen in lovely things! I want to go out secretly!'

'To meet a young man?' Mab's eyes sparkled suddenly.

'Of course! You can have my Sunday gown. It's clean, and it's plain enough.' Already she was running to the door.

Elaine picked up her hand-mirror when the girl had gone and stared at her face. Her eyes were unnaturally bright, her pale skin flushed. Yes, perhaps she did look as though she were going to an assignation. She drew a deep breath, put down the mirror and went to look out of the window. If only that were true! It must be wonderful to have a lover.

The shadows were lengthening across the grass, painting deeper colours across the formal beds. Birdsong filled the air, and the scent of early honeysuckle and roses drifted up to her window.

Mab's dress made them both laugh. Two of Elaine could have fitted into the ample waist, even with the lacings tight as they would go. But with the aid of a long, plaited girdle and a tightly-tied apron they managed the transformation. Mab brushed out Elaine's hair and knotted it beneath a snowy cap, and she was ready. Taking her darkest cloak, Elaine tiptoed down the staircase and fled towards the stables.

The grooms were idling over a game of loggats, lazily pitching sticks at a stake they had stuck into the dry ground, and showed little interest in her change of costume. Grumbling quietly, old Ned Potten detached himself from the game, saddled Elaine's black mare Cressid, and led the animal out to her.

'You see she don't put a foot in a rabbit-hole; that light is going fast,' he said grumpily, as he tossed her up into the saddle. Then, to her relief, he turned back to his game without suggesting that one of them accompany her.

It was quite dark in the grassy lanes which led from King's Brook towards the coast. Hedges of oak and foaming hawthorn met above her head, cutting out the bright evening light as Elaine skirted round to the south of Woodbridge, not wanting to ride through the steep, narrow, noisy streets of the town or along the quayside with its attendant lounging sailors.

She rode slowly, glimpsing the water through the trees. Pale bands of silver streaked the surface with carmine and

gold reflections from the sky, while the wind stirred in
the heavy canopy of leaves as she slipped from the high
saddle.

Tethering Cressid, she gathered up her skirts and walked
towards the edge of the trees to look down a small sandy
cliff into the creek. Sure enough, a ship lay there in the lee
of the woods, her spars in black silhouette against the
gilded water.

There was no sign of life on deck. Elaine drew back
slightly behind a huge old Scots pine and contemplated the
scene, uncertain what to do next.

Her courage was failing her fast. The thought of boarding
the graceful caravel, deserted though she looked, to seek
Tom among cut-throats and thieves suddenly lost its
appeal. She glanced up and down the beach, praying she
would see Tom approaching, her heart aching with misery
at the thought of missing him after she had come so far,
as, cautiously, she crept to the very edge of the low cliff,
clutching a branch to steady herself.

She was leaning out as far as she dared, when, without
warning, the sand beneath her feet gave way and with a
scream of terror she fell into space.

Desperately she flung out her arms, trying to save herself, her full skirts tangling between her legs as she
scrabbled for a foothold, but her fist closed on air as her
fingers missed their grasp and the branches of the trees
swung out of reach.

Then a man's hand was there, clamped on her wrist, and
another round her waist, and even as she began to fall she
was swung back from the cliff edge, sobbing with fear.

'You mustn't throw yourself away like that, my pretty,'
a rough voice whispered in her ear. 'That would be an
awful waste, that would. Now, what are you spying on so
quietly, I wonder?'

And she found herself being pulled round violently to
face her rescuer.

Elaine struggled to free herself, but she was held fast,
and she stared up at the man who had saved her, unable
to move. He was a man in his middle years, dressed in a
stained leather doublet and breeches, his hands and face

as tanned and scarred as the hide he wore. A naked cutless was thrust through his belt.

'Fancy your chances with the sailor boys, do you, my pretty?' He grinned at her, not slackening his grip.

She shook her head, too shocked for a moment to speak.

'Then what?' His eyes, deep set in the harsh face, were shrewd and not unkind as they scanned her. 'You don't look like a tavern wench.'

At last she found her tongue. 'My brother is down there on the ship,' she stammered. 'I wanted to say farewell to him, that's all.'

'Your brother?' He threw back his head and laughed. 'That's a new one! And who might your brother be?'

She was too frightened to lie. 'Tom. Tom Howard. Please will you tell him I'm here. I must speak to him!' She broke off, gazing pleadingly into his eyes.

He nodded slowly. 'Maybe you are speaking the truth. I can see a look of him in you. So you came to see *Black Witch* off and catch a glimpse of your brother's cronies, did you?'

'I must see him. Please?' She stopped, as a faint whistle sounded from the ship, echoing up through the trees on the still air. As if obedient to it, a faint ripple stirred on the water and she felt the wind touch her cheek once more. He turned and glanced down. 'It's too late, missie. That's "All hands aboard." We catch the tide, and the ship will be moving any minute. You wave your goodbyes to your brother from here, if you must, but don't let Kemp see you. He doesn't care for fond farewells!'

'Please,' she grabbed his arm. 'I must. Tom and I quarrelled and I didn't wish him luck. Please!' She paused as the man looked at her white face, and she knew it was useless to plead. 'At least tell him I'm sorry,' she whispered. 'Tell him I didn't mean it, and that I do wish him well.'

He nodded soberly. 'I dare say I'll manage that.' And, with a wink, he turned and began to climb down the cliff.

Elaine leant against the tree, defeated, watching as two more figures detached themselves from the undergrowth and made their way aboard. The ship had not been as

deserted as she looked; dozens of silent figures had
appeared at the foot of the masts, and running nimbly up
into the rigging as the gangplank was hauled inboard, but
there was still no sign of Tom.

Disappointed, she turned away and began to walk along
the point towards the river, following the cliff edge. In
places, the sandy soil had partially collapsed, and she began
carefully to climb down the crumbling escarpment, sliding,
and clinging to torn roots and branches, the loose sand
filling her shoes.

Near the bottom, she lost her footing and tumbled to
the soft jumble of soil and sand. Bruised, she rose to her
feet slowly, glancing round to make sure she had not been
observed. She gasped. *Black Witch*, drifting silently with
the tide towards the mouth of the creek, held fore and aft
by warps to the shore, had come level with her. As she
looked up towards the towering deck, a line of grinning
faces peered at her from the bulwarks. Then the high
sterncastle of the ship was abreast of her, and she could
make out the features of the sailor who had accosted her
at the top of the cliff, and another. Almost irresistibly
her eyes were drawn to the second man, and she knew
instinctively that this must be Guy Kemp, Tom's partner,
the captain of the ship.

The tanned, handsome features, long straight nose and
square jaw were framed by the wild tangle of flame-gold
hair and beard. She stared at him, shivering, unable to
drag her eyes away. Never had she seen so attractive a
man—or one who looked so cruel.

His gaze raked her as his ship drifted silently past. For
a moment their eyes met, and she felt his sardonic glance
hold hers. She could not breathe, and her mouth went dry.
Then his white teeth flashed as he began to laugh, and she
knew that he, like all his crew, must have seen her fall.
Mockingly, he raised his hand in salute before turning
away.

She fled up the beach, careless now of who saw her,
ducking beneath the willow and aspen to cut across to the
main river and the footpath. Her cheeks were burning with
indignation, and her breath caught in her throat as she

rounded the corner and lost sight of the ship. Only then could she try to calm herself and straighten her cloak. It would be full dusk before *Black Witch* dropped her towing-warps and turned out into the main river. Then she could look for one last time unobserved at the ship which carried Tom away and at the man whose eyes had caused such a strange turbulence in her breast.

When the tall figure in black accosted Elaine on the river bank, she nearly died of fright. She had time only to see that he was broad-shouldered and dark, and that his doublet was trimmed with silver lace, before she ducked away from him and ran. Behind her, she heard him hesitate for an instant, and in that time she had gained the trees and found Cressid. She threw herself on to the horse and allowed it to pick its way along the rutted path through the trees.

She did not draw rein until she was a couple of miles away, slowing to a standstill on the edge of the heath. When she held her breath and listened, there was no sound of pursuit.

Trying to steady herself as she set the mare towards King's Brook at a sedate walk, she felt nothing but sharp bitterness and misery. Far behind her, Tom was well on his way without her ever having caught a single glimpse of him, while instead she had been seen and ridiculed by the entire crew of *Black Witch*, including her captain. At the sudden thought of Guy Kemp's mocking gaze, the blood began to drum once more in her temples, eclipsing completely the fear she had felt when the stranger challenged her. It was as if she could feel again the strange power of Kemp's glance. Furious at her own foolishness, she tried to change the drift of her thoughts as she urged Cressid on. She would look forward, she comforted herself, to telling Tom exactly what she thought of his Captain Kemp!

She was home and already half undressed when the door of her bedroom opened and Mab slipped into the room.

'Why, Mistress Elaine!' The girl started visibly. 'I didn't know you were back. Why are you in here with only one candle? Look at you!' Scolding, she bustled about fetching fresh candles for the sconces, closing the heavy shutters against the moonrise, and taking an embroidered gown from the press.

'No, Mab. Not my clothes. I just want to go to bed,' Elaine protested. 'It's late.'

'I know, my love.' Mab had instantly noticed her mistress's pale face. 'Near midnight, I'd guess. But I'm afraid you must go downstairs to your father. He's been asking for you since supper.' She picked up the discarded dress and apron, not commenting on the sand-stains as she folded them. Briskly she helped Elaine to dress, not giving her time to argue, and pushed her out of the room.

Elaine ran. Her father was sitting in his library, poring over a map spread on the table. He looked up as she let herself into the room and dropped a deep curtsy in the doorway.

'Papa dearest? I'm sorry. I didn't know you wanted me. I was in the still-room earlier, and then I was so tired I went straight up to bed.' She adapted the truth a little, not liking to lie to her father.

His hard face relaxed into a smile. 'It is Thomas I want, daughter.' He straightened and walked to the fireplace, where a log was burning in spite of the warmth of the night. 'I guessed you might know where he was. No one else seems to.'

Elaine went white. She looked away quickly, unable to meet her father's eye. 'I haven't seen him since last night, Papa.' To admit that he had come to her room at dawn would have been as good as confessing that she knew his secret.

Robert Howard squinted at her shrewdly, and sniffed. 'You are quite sure you don't know?'

'Quite sure.'

He sighed testily. 'Off wenching with his cronies again, I suppose! I only hope he returns by tomorrow. We have an important visitor whom I want him to meet and work with. Sir Edward Brandon.' He eyed her thoughtfully, gnawing his knuckle. 'I particularly want you to meet him, my dear. He is unmarried, and, I hear, looking for a bride.'

Elaine gasped, all thought of Tom forgotten. 'Papa, you promised I need not marry unless I chose the man myself!'

'True, child. But you are too slow in choosing. You will soon be past the age when you should be married.' He walked stiffly to the table and poured a glass of wine. 'What are you? Twenty? Your poor mother had borne and lost two children already at your age. But there, I have said I'll not force you, and I don't wish to, but you begin to try my patience.' He shook his head sadly. 'I blame myself for not marrying again when your mother died, Elaine. Tom and you should have had more brothers and sisters, and another mother to raise you; to keep order and to bring some light and joy to this house.'

There was a moment's silence.

Elaine saw her father's tears, and knew that he was thinking of the tomb in the church across the garden with the stone effigy of her mother and the five small figures beside her of her own brothers and sisters, none of whom had survived infancy.

Taking a deep draught of wine, Robert Howard walked with deliberate steps back to the fireplace. 'I met Sir Edward in London, although he lives only some twenty miles from here at Aldebourne,' he said thoughtfully. 'Ostensibly he is here to buy stores for the King.'

'Ostensibly?' Elaine had seated herself nervously on the high-backed settle near the fire.

He gave a tight smile. 'He has to have a reason for being in Woodbridge that would give him access to all the warehouses and ships round here. At my request, Sir Edward has the King's commission to seek out and exterminate these pirates who have been preying on our ships over the past eighteen months. Things cannot go on as they have been. It is quite obvious that these rogues are based somewhere near here, and I mean to have their heads nailed to the town gates!'

He had not noticed Elaine's stillness, or the pallor of her skin as she stared, horrified, at him. 'Papa . . .' she spoke at last, her voice husky with terror. 'Surely the merchants of Woodbridge can guard their own ships? They have no need of an outsider.'

'I told you, girl, he is not an outsider. He's Suffolk born like ourselves, and is experienced in these matters; he's acted as pirate-catcher to the King before, rooting out nests of the varmints down in Cornwall and Dorset. No, he's the man we need.' He rubbed his thin hands together and held them out to the smouldering logs. 'Good-looking, too.' He gave her a sly glance. 'You'll like him, daughter.'

Elaine did not hear the last comment. Her mind was spinning as she thought of Tom, Sir Edward's possible designs on herself momentarily forgotten. Somehow she had to warn him. She got to her feet, making towards the door, still reeling with the shock of what he had said. 'Papa, if you will forgive me, it is late and I'm tired.'

'Of course, child.' He grinned to himself. Mention a handsome man, and the girl skittered off like a frightened filly!

Elaine closed the door behind her and walked, dazed, towards the staircase, her father's words echoing in her ears. He meant to have the pirates' heads nailed to the town gates. And one of those pirates was Tom!

Letting herself into her bedroom, she leaned against the oak panelling and took a deep breath, numb with fear. She had to get word to Tom. Sitting at her table, she cudgelled her brain to remember the name of the tavern Tom had mentioned where they would know about the whereabouts of *Black Witch*. She had to help Tom; then he, in his turn, would help her to be rid of yet another unwelcome suitor.

She frowned at the thought, wishing to convince herself that there was nothing to fear and that this man, Sir Edward Brandon, would be rebuffed as easily as the others, but she could no longer be entirely certain.

Silently Mab let herself into the room, carrying a pitcher of warm water. She looked sympathetically at Elaine, guessing some of what had been said in the library. The linenfold panelling on the door was thin, and the ears of the steward, David Churchman, had been long as he passed down the passage outside. It had not taken him long to relay to the kitchens what he had heard.

'Shall I help you to undress, mistress?' Her voice was unusually gentle.

Elaine turned with a start. 'I never heard you come in! Yes, Mab, I am tired.' She stood still as the maid unfastened the lacings at the back of her gown.

'I reckoned you'd want to go straight to bed now,' the girl went on, pulling expertly at the stiffened fabric until it fell rustling around Elaine's knees.

She looked up wearily. Mab was right. The only thing to do now was to go to bed and sleep. Tom would be far out to sea. Perhaps tomorrow, when the sun was high and her wits were about her, she would be better able to decide what to do when he returned.

In spite of the lateness of the hour she lay awake for a long time, however, tossing and turning feverishly on the deep feather bed, haunted by her fears of this unknown man whom Robert Howard had unwittingly hired to ensnare his own son. But when at last she drifted into an uneasy sleep, it was not Tom's face she saw in her dreams, nor that of her suitor, his unknown prosecutor. It was the face which had stared down at her from the ship that had carried her brother into the darkness; the cruel, handsome, haunted face of the man who had laughed when she fell almost at his feet in the sand—the face of the pirate captain, Kemp.

The great hall, the main room in the large, lavishly furnished house, was used as a dining-hall now only for very special occasions. But next day Robert Howard had invited the leading merchants and landowners in the area to meet his guest, and the tables were being set out early. Elaine did not see Sir Edward arrive. Mab was brushing her hair and coiling it beneath the elaborate head-dress that complemented her stiff pale blue gown and heavily embroidered kirtle when he rode up to the front of the house, and she could see nothing from her windows. Mab, however, was a mine of information.

'He's tall, and ever so dark, and really quite handsome; but he's not come to stay. His traps are at a tavern in Stone Street, so Hal says. He hasn't even brought a boy with him.'

Elaine breathed a sigh of relief. To have him as a guest

under their very roof would have proved too great a strain
for her. She was calmer and more rational this morning.
Was Sir Edward, after all, so great a threat? He had no
way of knowing that Tom was involved; he had come to
King's Brook not because he suspected Tom, but because
her father had asked him to. The son of the house would be
the last person on earth he would suspect. The knowledge
made her almost cheerful as she watched her reflection in
the mirror while Mab fastened a jewelled pendant round
her neck. And as for the threat of his being forced on her
as a husband—her father had never insisted yet, and she
was confident she could persuade him, once more, that she
was more useful to him at home than ever she would be as
another man's wife.

'You look quite lovely, mistress,' Mab said, when at last
she was ready. 'I should think every man there will fall in
love with you.'

Elaine smiled. So Mab knew that their guest was unmarried and in the market for a wife. She wondered whether
there was anything at all that the servants in the house did
not know, and she raised her eyes to meet Mab's innocent
blue ones. How many of them knew that Tom sailed on
*Black Witch*?

She could hear the rumble of male voices before she
reached the turn of the stair which led down into the great
hall, and paused to summon up her courage before she
began to descend the last flight, conscious of some dozen
faces raised towards her as she walked slowly down. Her
father held out his hands, as he made his way towards her.
'Here she is at last, my lovely Elaine. Sweetheart, you
know Thomas Seckford, Ned Wolsey, Cousin Richard—
in fact I think you know everyone except our special guest.
Come, meet Sir Edward Brandon. Sir, this is my daughter
Elaine.'

Overcome suddenly with nervousness, Elaine took the
outstretched hand and curtsied to the ground as the conversation resumed around her and a burst of laughter floated
over her head. Only as she rose gracefully once more did
she look up at the face of the man who still held her fingers
so lightly in his.

The silver lace trimming to the doublet was the same; only, this time, the doublet was midnight blue, not black. She was intensely aware of her father standing expectantly at Sir Edward's elbow, watching, as she finally met his gaze. It was the man who had tried to catch her the night before on the shores of the Deben: the stranger who had been observing *Black Witch* sail.

# CHAPTER
## TWO

THERE WAS no sign of recognition, however, in the deep-set brown eyes as, smiling, Sir Edward raised her hand to his lips. 'Mistress Elaine, this is indeed an honour.'

With a silent prayer of thanks that he had obviously not seen her clearly in the dark at Kingston Point, she murmured a few quiet words of welcome, drawing her hand away as soon as she could. Under cover of the general conversation, she studied him. He was tall and well built; in his early thirties, she guessed. His features were even, strongly drawn beneath dark brown hair, but he was not handsome; striking, perhaps, but his eyes were too calculating, his mouth too hard. She felt a strange revulsion.

As their guests crowded close to him, impressed with the competence with which he discussed the King's trading policies, a matter of passionate interest to them, Elaine quietly withdrew to the window embrasure, trying to compose her thoughts. It could have been no coincidence that Edward Brandon had been at Kingston watching *Black Witch* sail. He had been in Woodbridge for only a few hours, and already he had pinpointed the ship. She bit her lip in an agony of anguish before glancing back towards their guests, all soberly dressed in furs and silks; all important figures who would stop at nothing to see that their trade was unhindered. And, at their centre, this tall, observant man who was the King's pirate-catcher.

Her eyes went automatically to his face, and she met his speculative gaze, which had followed her to the window. Colouring sharply, she looked away, but not before she had seen his stern features relax into the suspicion of a triumphant smile.

She was seated between Sir Edward and her father at dinner, saying very little as the conversation sparked back and forth. There was talk of trade and wool and war, of the likelihood of a good harvest, of politics, and of the court of King Henry and his Spanish queen, Katherine, and then of more trade as the courses of the meal came and went: broths and stews, pies and fishes, cockerels, peacocks, lamb, quince pie and custards and marchpane.

As she sipped slowly from the delicate Venetian glass into which the wine had been served on this special occasion, she longed for the meal to be over.

'I'd have wished my son to be here,' her father said suddenly to their guest of honour, 'to meet you straight away and give you his help, but these young blades are all the same. Take your eyes off them for a minute, and they are off wenching or bear-baiting or losing good money at the dice!'

Elaine swallowed a little gasp, and then prayed that Sir Edward had not heard her. If he had, he gave no sign. 'I'll meet your son soon enough, I dare say,' he reassured his host affably. 'And I'll work him hard then, have no fear! Let him enjoy himself while he can.' He glanced at her with a smile.

At the sight of her white face, his eyes lingered thoughtfully on her. A moment before, he had imagined her at last beginning to relax in his company, but now she was as tense as ever. He frowned. There was much to intrigue him about Elaine Howard. Inwardly he gave a grim chuckle. He had not expected to find the girl from Kingston Point so easily. That she should be the daughter of one of the richest of the pirate's victims had taken him aback for a moment or two when he met her, but he had not betrayed the fact that he recognised her and he had seen her fear and embarrassment slowly subside; already one or two of the pieces in the puzzle were falling into place. Elaine would be in a position to pass on the information about cargoes and sailing dates; he wondered whether she was really the innocent victim of an unscrupulous man, not even knowing what his true trade was.

The girl was quite beautiful. Her ash-blonde hair and clear skin gave her a sense of fragile loveliness which caused his breath to catch. He thought for an instant of

the list of rich heiresses he had drawn up in an idle moment
in his room at the King's palace at Greenwich: potential
wives, every one. How strange that Elaine Howard, whose
name topped that list, should be mixed up somehow with
the very piracy he had come to eradicate. But it did not
matter; probably she was being used. If it were more than
that, if she had a lover among the pirate crew, all the more
reason to track them down and ensure that every one of
them paid the full penalty of the law. He smiled quietly to
himself. Watching her lover swing would add spice to his
wooing.

When at last the meal was over, Elaine excused herself
as soon as she could and left the great hall where her father
would continue to entertain his guests for the best part of
the afternoon.

Her mind was fixed on one thing: she had to find the
tavern and warn Tom that *Black Witch* was under suspicion. Snatching her cloak, she let herself quietly out of
a side door of the house and ran. When she glanced over
her shoulder towards the house, there was no sign of life.

Under the hot afternoon sky, the gardens were deserted
except for one of the weeding-women bent over the beds
of hyssop and roses. Through the stable arch she could
hear the bees in the clover of the paddocks behind the
stables. Cressid was fresh, jibbing at the bit, her hooves
dancing sideways through clouds of bluebells, but Elaine
hardly saw the beauty of the afternoon around her. Her
mind was fixed on her task.

She left the horse at Goody Cattermole's house in New
Street, and headed towards the market place, holding her
skirts clear of the filthy cobbles. The town was full of
jostling crowds and the rattle of wheels as laden wagons
swayed up the narrow streets between the jettied houses.

Her brain was whirling as she stared at the shops and
taverns, searching for the King's Head. Then she saw it;
the carved sign was half hidden behind the tailgate of an
abandoned wagon. Without giving herself time to think,
she opened the door. Inside, some half-dozen men were
seated round a table, staring at a sheaf of lading-bills. They
looked up as she entered.

Elaine looked at the man nearest her, judging by his filthy apron and the tray beneath his arm that he must be the host. She cleared her throat, forgetting to be cautious; all she wanted was to be gone. 'Please, can you help me? I'm seeking news of a ship called *Black Witch*. Do you know when she will return?'

The man stared at her with blank, insolent eyes. 'Never heard of her, my pretty. Whose vessel would she be?' Slowly he put down his tray, and took a step towards her. 'Stopped away too long, has he, my dear? Maybe we can supply you with what's missing from your life . . .'

'No!' Elaine backed away from him towards the door. 'You don't understand! The ship belongs to my brother. He gave me this address and said I could ask here.'

'And what is your brother's name, lady?' Another man looked up, bored, from the documents.

She hesitated, not wanting to use Tom's name. But whose could she give? She felt increasingly panic-stricken as all six faces now grinned insolently up at her.

'Kemp,' she said desperately. 'It's Kemp's ship.'

The atmosphere in the shadowy room became suddenly tense. The standing man moved another step towards her threateningly.

'What do you know of Guy Kemp, lady?' he whispered hoarsely. 'With your fine clothes and your dainty complexion.' He pulled at her cloak contemptuously. 'You're no sister to Guy, lady!'

Behind him, one of his companions sniggered. 'They're all sisters under their clothes, Wilf.'

Elaine looked from one to the other, her cheeks flaming. 'No, you don't understand! I'm *Tom's* sister. I only want to know when the ship will berth. Please!' She had her back to the door.

'I see. You are Tom's sister!' The seated man lunged towards her and grabbed her wrist. 'Well, I reckon it doesn't matter whose sister you are. There's time enough for you to pleasure us a bit before *Black Witch* returns and still be ready for your Tom when he gets back.'

Struggling frantically to free herself from him, Elaine kicked out at the man's ankles in a panic as a quiet voice from the table cut through the general laughter.

'Let her go, Tad. Whatever she is to the men on *Black Witch*, you'll not want to tangle with Kemp when he returns. He's more likely to put a dagger in your gizzard and ask questions after if you mess about with one of his women!'

Tad dropped her wrist as if it had burnt him, and Elaine staggered back trying to restrain her tears. At the table, the man who had spoken last stared at her thoughtfully. 'Don't come here again, ever, Tom's sister. Do you understand? And don't go anywhere else to ask about *Black Witch*. This town keeps its secrets close.' He gave a grim smile. 'For what it's worth, they might come in on the night tide tomorrow, but then again they might not. That's all we know.'

Not stopping to thank him, she opened the door and dived back into the blinding sunshine of the street. From within, she heard a gale of coarse laughter. Trembling with relief and humiliation, she began to return down the hill to reclaim her horse, and only a tall shadow that fell directly across her path made her stop.

Sir Edward Brandon was standing in front of her. 'Mistress Howard! How strange that I should meet you here.' He bowed, his eyes searching her face. 'I had thought you to say you were going to rest after dinner.'

She felt her colour heighten even more, as anger surged through her. 'I changed my mind, Sir Edward. I was not aware that you wanted to know my whereabouts!'

He gave a tight smile. 'It hardly seems proper that Robert Howard's daughter should be running about the streets of Woodbridge in full view of half the town without so much as a maid to attend her,' he said coolly. 'I cannot believe that your father would approve of such conduct, mistress.'

Her amber eyes were blazing. 'Whether or not my father approves of my conduct, sir, is hardly your business! Now, if you will excuse me, I wish to pass.'

She took a step towards him, but he did not move. 'May I ask what business you had in that tavern?' he demanded suddenly. She could feel his eyes on her face.

'What tavern?' She had to bluff her way out of his trap. 'I visit no taverns, sir, I assure you! I have been to see a friend; her name is no concern of yours.' Anger and indignation gave her courage as she stared at him. 'Did you follow me from home?'

To her immense satisfaction, he began to look slightly disconcerted. 'It appears that I must have,' he said coldly.

'Then I am sorry you should have had so boring a journey!' This time, as she moved forward, he stood aside to let her pass. Her eyes had deepened to the colour of topaz, and her pale cheeks were alive with the touch of blood beneath her skin. Had she but known it, the face which glared so furiously at Edward Brandon as she swept past him was one of passionate beauty.

She walked swiftly down the hill, and only when she reached the gate of the stable where Cressid waited did she glance around. Sir Edward had not followed her.

There was no sign of Sir Edward that evening, to her immense relief, when Elaine joined her father for their evening meal in the small supper-room beside his library. The two of them were alone.

Robert Howard was ill at ease and cross, but he had already forgotten his daughter's over-hasty departure from the great hall after dinner, and was once more thinking irritably about his son. 'It is too bad of Thomas! I need him here with me.' He coughed, his hand pressed against his side dramatically. 'I want someone to represent me at the warehouse tomorrow when Brandon begins his ordering.'

'But, Papa!' Elaine stared at him. 'I thought that was a pretence. He is here as a spy, not to purchase goods for the King!'

Robert looked at her sharply. 'A spy! That is a strange word to use. Whatever his purpose here, Elaine, he does mean to buy for the King, and I'm not strong enough to go down to the town to supervise. Not yet.'

'But your cough is better, Papa.' Elaine smiled coaxingly. 'And Tom will soon return. Wherever he is, he will be back before long. I'm sure of it.'

Robert nodded wearily, pushing his plate away. 'I'm sure you're right. But, anyway, things will be easier from tomorrow. I have told Sir Edward to pack his chests and come here as our guest. He said at the start that he wanted to stay in the town with his ear to the ground, but now he feels he can do just as well from King's Brook. I think he has found an attraction here he had not dared to expect,' he chuckled.

'Not me, Papa, I hope?'

'Of course you, you silly child! It's certainly not Mabbet! Sir Edward is showing great interest in you and you should be glad of it. A fine-looking man like that!'

Elaine blushed violently. 'Papa, I have told you. I have no wish to consider any man yet.'

'Pish!' He banged the tankard down. 'I'll not allow much more of this childish modesty. You think about him, and think about him well, my girl. And, for once, Tom will agree with me. It is time you were married!'

As she lay in bed that night, her father's words streamed through Elaine's head, filling her with foreboding. The dark, unpleasant presence of Sir Edward Brandon was beginning to haunt her. Just how much did he know of Tom's ship and her crew, and why had he followed her that afternoon to the tavern in the square? Could he have recognised her as the girl he had seen at Kingston Point? Surely he would have shown some sign?

Sir Edward arrived early the next morning, accompanied by two servants and a pack-horse. He was shown to the finest guest-room in the west wing before joining Master Robert for refreshment in his library. Elaine refused to leave her room.

'Tell Papa I am not well,' she instructed Mab. It was almost true. After her sleepless night, her eyes were heavy and her head throbbed painfully as she lay on the bed. She wanted the day to pass as quickly as possible; at nightfall she was going to slip out once more and ride to Kingston Hill to await the return of *Black Witch*.

The day passed interminably. Mab reported that Robert Howard had had himself carried into Woodbridge in a

litter so that he could supervise the choice of goods on Sir
Edward's list, and the two, obviously fast becoming friends,
had returned only in time for the evening meal. Her
presence had been sorely missed, Mab added darkly, and
Elaine smiled a little, thinking of her father's fury that she
was not there to flirt with their visitor.

At noon she had finally fallen asleep and slept for several
hours. When she awoke, her head was clear. Restored by
a tray of bread and meat and a posset of milk curdled in
sweet wine, she began to feel almost cheerful. Mab giggled
on hearing that her mistress was about to make another
mysterious visit to the town, but was greatly relieved that
she did not once more claim her Sunday gown. Instead
Elaine selected one of her own, a full-skirted high-waisted
dress of deep burgundy silk worn over a cream kirtle. She
reached for the key to her jewel chest and threw back the
lid. Tom's packet of letters lay there on top, and gently
she touched his scrawled, almost illegible writing with her
fingertip before pushing it aside and selecting a heavy ruby
necklace. She clipped it round her throat, then, closing the
casket, turned away to wrap herself in her green velvet
cloak. Briefly she wondered why she should be dressing so
carefully for her dangerous lonely ride to Kingston, but
deep down she knew it might have more than a little to do
with the thought of confronting Tom beneath the sardonic
gaze of the captain of *Black Witch*.

Mab waited with her in her room until the house had
fallen silent. The three-quarter moon had floated clear of
the yew hedge and Elaine could see across the garden as
though it were daylight. Drawing the bed-curtains to
deceive anyone glancing through the door, she picked up
a candle and beckoned Mab to follow her. The two girls
crept through into the empty bedroom beyond Elaine's,
which lay at the very end of the house, where beneath a
tapestry wall-hanging, a small door led to a forgotten
narrow stair that she and Tom had used since childhood to
escape their nurses. Tom still used it when he wished to
leave the house unobserved. Elaine led the way, the candle
held high before her, and at the bottom, she paused before
the small door in the outside wall of the house. It was

heavily bolted. Mab was close behind her, her eyes huge in the candlelight. 'Take the candle, Mab, while I open it.' Her hands were trembling as she forced back the bolts and dragged the door ajar, peering out into the moonlight through the curtain of ivy which hung across it. Looking back at Mab, she put her finger to her lips.

'Don't lock it behind me,' she breathed. 'Go back, and go to bed. I'll see you in the morning.'

Tiptoeing over the grass, she headed for the stables. She did not notice Sir Edward Brandon sitting on the low moss-covered wall until she was a few feet from him. He had risen as he saw her, and walked swiftly to intercept her.

'Well met, sweetheart! I am glad to see you have recovered from your megrims,' he said quietly. His fingers on her forearm were tight enough to prevent her from pulling away from him.

'Sir Edward! You startled me!'

He looked down into the wide eyes, taking in the velvet cloak and the glowing gems at her throat. So, the little trollop was off to another meeting with her pirate lover. He smiled grimly; his information too had been that *Black Witch* would return that night.

'You seem bound for an assignation, my dear,' he went on softly. His fingers had not relinquished their hold on her arm. 'I wonder who the lucky man can be?' His voice was smooth.

Her mouth had gone dry, and her mind, stunned for a moment by the shock of meeting him, began to race. She tried to make herself relax beneath his grasp, looking at him as warmly as she could. 'Indeed, Sir Edward, I only hoped for an assignation. And I think I have found it.' Her lips were stiff as she forced herself to smile.

She felt his fingers loosen slightly on her arm. 'I hope you don't think me too forward! I was looking out at the moonlight from my window up there, and I saw you . . .' She looked down, unable to go on with the lie.

The house lay in darkness, and somewhere near by a peacock screamed, disturbed by their presence. Elaine gasped at the sound, stepping involuntarily backward with

a shiver. Sir Edward caught hold of her once more. 'Not
so fast, my dear! I have something to say to you.'

She looked up at him, suddenly afraid again. 'I must go
back, Sir Edward. I should not have come out here . . .'

'Yet you did. You came to see me.' Both hands were on
her arms now. He was drawing her to him, enjoying the
fear and anger he saw as his mouth drew near hers.

At the touch of his lips, she dragged herself away from
him, shuddering with revulsion. 'Sir Edward! You forget
yourself!'

He was laughing at her now, standing, arms folded, as
he watched her.

'I doubt if my father would find it amusing, sir, if I told
him that a guest under his roof had forced himself on
me.'

'Oh come, Elaine,' he sneered. 'I didn't force you. You
can't pretend that was the first time you have been kissed.
I doubt your moonlit tryst had anything to do with me at
all. A groom, was it? Or a farm boy? Rumour has it that
your tastes run very low!'

Stung to silence by his sarcasm, she stared at him. Colour
flared in her cheeks for an instant, and then she felt herself
grow pale. 'How dare you!'

He had seated himself on the wall now, and his face was
insolent with amusement. 'You were going to the stables,
weren't you? To see a groom? Or was it just to fetch a
horse, perhaps—to ride to your lover?'

'No!'

'Then you really were coming out to meet me?'

'No!' She took a few steps away from him. 'No, I was
not. I merely wished for some air.'

'Some air?' He echoed her mockingly. 'And, for some
air, you dress in silks and put on your finest jewellery.' He
gestured contemptuously at her necklace. 'You honour the
moon, perhaps? Or the nightingale, with your best clothes?
Come, Elaine, why not tell me who he is?'

Elaine stared at him for a moment, then, all thoughts of
going to Tom banished from her mind, she began to run
back towards the house, intent only on reaching safety
before Sir Edward laid hands on her again. She ran past

the little hidden door, instinctively not wanting him to see it, slipping round the corner to the front of the house.

Sir Edward had not moved. He watched the flying shadow of the girl in her dark cloak as she sped out of sight. Beauty, spirit and money. Oh yes, he would enjoy making Elaine Howard his wife, once he had disposed of the crew of *Black Witch*.

# CHAPTER
# THREE

THE FRONT door was unlocked; Sir Edward must have let himself out by it to go into the garden. With relief Elaine pushed it open, her hands shaking in her haste as she fumbled with the heavy iron latch, and slipped into the great hall. She crept through deserted bedrooms until she reached the small one next to her own where Mab slept. Straining her eyes in the darkness of the shuttered room, she looked towards her recumbent form. Mab was obviously fast asleep.

In her own room there was enough moonlight to see, just. She felt about for her tinder-box, nearly dropping the flint in her agitation as she groped to light a candle, her heart still pounding with fear and anger. Sir Edward had insulted her and taken liberties with her, and worse than either of these, he had stopped her going to Tom. With a sigh of relief she had the candle lit at last, and she ran to the window and cautiously peered out between the shutters. The garden was still as bright as day. Below, on the grass, Sir Edward was pacing slowly up and down between the beds. He appeared to be deep in thought. With an exclamation of anger, she left the window. It was as though he suspected her, as though he deliberately intended to stop her leaving the house. She sat down on the end of the bed. Had he, after all, seen her at Kingston Point? Did that explain his insulting remark about her fondness for low company? In spite of her anger, an irresistible urge to giggle bubbled up in her throat. So, he imagined that she had a lover on the ship!

She rose and went back to the window, her amusement gone as soon as it had come. Whatever his reasons for being there, he was keeping her from Tom. From the shelter of the shutters, she watched the figure pacing the gardens, still seething with resentment as she saw him methodically walk towards the stables and back.

There was only one entrance to the stable-yard, and without using it, she could not reach Cressid. Briefly she debated trying to catch one of the horses out in the distant paddocks, but she dismissed the idea almost at once. The harness was all in the stables, and she doubted if she could catch one unaided at night.

Frustrated, she paced the room, glancing out each time she approached the window. But each time he was still there, and the last time she looked, he was standing immediately below her window, staring up. She moved quickly out of sight, and furiously sat down on her bed once more, determined to wait.

She did not realise that she had fallen asleep until she woke with a jerk to find herself perched uncomfortably at the end of her bed. Puzzled by the sudden darkness outside, she saw that the moon had risen further and was now soaring behind the tall, twisted chimneys of the house. Wearily she rose and stretched her arms above her head. The tide must have long ago been full; had *Black Witch* come tonight, she would already have berthed and her crew dispersed. It was too late to intercept Tom now.

With a heavy heart she reached up to unfasten the heavy jewels from her throat and dropped them on the table by the candle, then slowly she began to loosen the laces that fastened her gown. Stepping out of the deep red silk, she picked the dress up and threw it over a stool. Dressed in nothing but her fine white shift she went once more, almost from habit, to the window and peered out one last time. The gardens were still bright, the shadows foreshortened, but there was no sign of the patrolling figure now that it was too late for her to go to Tom. Sadly she turned to the bed, her eyes heavy with misery and exhaustion. In only seconds, she was once more asleep.

A sharp click in the next room woke her. It was a sudden awakening—one minute she was deeply asleep, the next wide awake, her heart pounding with fright. She sat up, her ears straining in the silence. She could just see the window faintly, the small leaded panes dimly silhouetted

against the starry sky. Beside her bed, the candle guttered
and smoked in a sudden draught as the door slowly opened.
Holding her breath, she stared as a figure materialised out
of the shadows and closed the door silently. In a second
she was out of bed, running in her thin shift towards him.

'Tom? Oh, Tom, thank God! He didn't see you, did he?
He's been waiting out there for hours, patrolling the stable,
watching my window. It's almost as if he knew . . .'

Her voice sank to an uncertain whisper as she reached
out her hand towards the figure. 'Tom? It is you?'

'No, mistress, it is not Tom.' The quiet voice that
answered her was deep and vibrant; the voice of a stranger.
'Please make no sound.'

Her gasp of surprise and fear was cut off as he stepped
towards her. In two strides he was past her and had reached
the candle. She caught a glimpse of the arrogant nose, the
burnished hair and beard, the watchful steel-blue eyes,
before he snuffed the dying flame and plunged the room
into total darkness. It was Guy Kemp.

Elaine backed away from him, her mouth suddenly dry
with fear as she heard the scrape of his heel on the boards.
He had turned to face her.

'You must keep silent, Mistress Howard. I have no wish
to cross swords with your watcher outside, whoever he
may be,' he said quietly. He went to the window and
looked out through the half-open shutters. Elaine could
see him now in the faint starlight as her eyes accustomed
themselves to the darkness. His mouth was set in a grim
line.

'How did you get in?' she stammered at last.

She saw his lips relax slightly into a sombre smile as he
turned towards her. 'Through the door. Tom told me about
your secret entrance beneath the ivy. How lucky it was
unbolted!' He glanced again at the window, stepping back
out of the faint starlight into the darkness of the shadows.
'Now, please light a new candle so that we can talk. I shall
close the shutters.'

Elaine ran to the table. With shaking hands she lifted
the still-warm candle-stump from its pricket and found a
new one to jam in its place. As the pale light flared and

steadied, she turned to look at her visitor. When he had fastened the shutters and drawn the heavy curtains, he came towards her, dressed in a rich deep-blue doublet and soft shirt. There was a cutlass at his waist. Vibrant power seemed to emanate from his body, and she began to shiver in spite of the warmth of the room.

He in his turn was scrutinising her in the candlelight, his eyes straying from her loosened hair and pale face to the fine gossamer shift which clung to her body. He bowed slightly. 'Perhaps I should introduce myself. I am Guy Kemp, master of *Black Witch*.'

She did not move. 'I know. I saw you the evening I came looking for Tom.'

His eyes became strangely enigmatic. 'Ah yes. You were lying on the sand; a veritable stranded mermaid.' He smiled gently. 'My crew were all in favour of rescuing you from your uncomfortable fate and carrying you out to sea with us.'

Elaine's cheeks coloured violently. 'The vulgar opinions of your crew don't interest me, sir,' she retorted, trying to counter the strange excitement which coursed through her. 'You have no business here. Where's Tom?'

He looked away from her abruptly. When he met her gaze again, the mocking humour was gone. His eyes were suddenly full of intense compassion.

A whisper of fear touched her. 'What is it?' she breathed. 'What has happened? Why are you here?'

For a moment he did not speak. She stared at him pleadingly, then rushed on, crying softly into the silence, 'It's Tom, isn't it? Something has happened to Tom!'

'He is dead, Elaine.' The deep voice was gentle.

'Dead?' she echoed, not understanding, not wanting to believe him.

But his expression told her the truth. She could not breathe. The room began to spin and sway, and she reached out to steady herself as her eyes filled with tears, blindly stepping towards the grim-faced man who stood before her, too overwhelmed with grief to know what she was doing.

His strong arms gathered her to him and he held her

close, her face pressed against his shirt, his fingers gently stroking her hair, comforting her, as if it were the most natural thing in the world for him to be standing there in her bedroom holding a half-naked girl in the candlelight.

There was the smell of the ship on him: the tar and the salt and the night sea air still clinging to his clothes; and, disquietingly, she could feel the iron-hard muscles of his chest and the strong beating of his heart beneath her cheek as her tears fell. 'How did he die? Why? What happened?' Her voice was muffled with sobs.

'We were alongside a Flemish galleon. We'd put a boarding-party on her. There seemed to be no resistance, then someone on the Fleming turned a mortar on us. Tom was wounded.' He hesitated, not wanting to tell her the truth—the blood and the agony as the young man's chest was blasted away, and the long minutes it had taken Tom to die in his arms. 'His last words were of you and your father. Then he said he loved you both.' He looked down at her sternly. 'He said, "Tell Elaine not to tell Papa how I died. Ever." '

She looked away from him, brushing her arm across her face and pushing her knuckles into her eyes in a vain attempt to stem the tears. Then suddenly she turned, her misery and despair overflowing into anger. 'How could you let it happen? How could you? With your cursed ship and your raids and your robbery! Tom would never hurt anyone! He had so much to live for . . .' She could not go on. Overwhelmed by a fresh torrent of sobbing, she flew at him, pounding his chest with her fists, wanting him to suffer as Tom had suffered, wanting to kill him with her bare hands.

Taken by surprise, it was a moment before he reacted. Then he caught her wrists with an oath and held her at arm's length. 'By Our Lady! Tom said you were a spitfire! I risk my life to tell you what happened because Tom asked me to come personally, and you attack me!' His hands on her wrists had the strength of steel. 'You are right,' he went on grimly. 'As the captain of my ship, I am responsible for the life of every man on her. I make no excuses. As to the profession we follow, Tom knew, as well as anyone, the risks as well as the rewards, and he enjoyed the danger!'

'*Enjoyed* it?' she exploded. 'How can you say that?'

'He came with us for the danger and the excitement, Elaine.' He gave a rueful scowl. 'It certainly wasn't for the money. He needed none of that, though he got his share, the same as every other man.'

He released her wrists abruptly. 'I loved him as a brother, too, so, when I say I am sorry for what has happened, I mean it. And I have no wish to cause you and your family more unhappiness than is necessary.' He swung away from her and stood staring down at the candle. 'Obviously you would wish his body brought home?'

'Yes.' Her choked whisper was barely audible.

'Then I shall have it done tomorrow. My men will be instructed to say he was attacked by footpads while on his way back here from a visit to London. It happens often enough.'

'Yes.'

'May I suggest that you tell your father yourself before they arrive? It would be kinder.'

'Kinder!' Her voice broke. 'Do you care how my father reacts, Master Kemp?'

'Tom cared.' His voice became suddenly forbidding. 'He cared a great deal for your father, and he told me that his health was precarious. If you care for him as much, you will try and prepare him for the shock. You may tell him that a servant of Tom's escaped and ran here to tell you what had happened.'

Elaine raised her hand, pressing it against her aching head. 'I don't understand. You are prepared to murder and rob, and yet you care about my father's health. It makes no sense!'

'Perhaps it would make more sense to you if I said I wanted your father alive for my own purposes,' he said harshly. 'You would believe that, I have no doubt.'

'Yes,' she said wearily after a moment. 'I would believe that of you, sir.'

'Then my next request will not surprise you.' He turned away so that his face was invisible again. 'For there is something further I have to discuss. I would not have mentioned it now, while you are still newly grieving for your brother, but it is urgent, and it may prove hard for me to speak to you alone again.'

Elaine stared at his silhouette, her indignation returning. 'I hope it will prove impossible for you to speak to me again, sir. Ever!'

He gave a quiet chuckle. 'Have you taken me in such dislike, then? Perhaps that is understandable. And there is no need, I assure you, for us to be friends; but colleagues we must be for a short while.'

'What do you mean?' She was beginning to tremble again. The restraint had gone from his voice, and she heard a new harshness there.

'I mean that there is something you have to do for me: a duty Tom was to have undertaken. As he can no longer help me, you must.'

He turned to her. 'I am sure you would wish to honour your brother's promises.' There was an undertone of menace in his voice now that frightened her, but she was determined not to show it.

'I think Tom has more than paid his debts to you, Master Kemp,' she retorted with as much spirit as she could muster, 'and paid dearly.'

'Perhaps he did,' he said harshly. 'Nevertheless, you must take his place, Mistress Elaine.'

'Take his place?' she echoed, her heart beating wildly.

'That is what I said. My plans are set; they depended on a meeting between Tom and a colleague of your father's to reassure him that he can return safely without waiting for an escort, and to discuss the date of his return to be set at my convenience.' He laughed grimly. 'Although our friend will no doubt be surprised to find a lady carrying the authority of the merchants of Woodbridge, I am sure he would not query the Howard seal and your name.'

'No!' Cold horror flooded through her at his words. 'No! How would you even suggest such a thing? With Tom's body not even cold, you think only of your pocket! You are . . . vile. *Vile*! I shall never help you. And Tom wouldn't have, either, I'm sure of it! Not against my father's friends . . .' But even as she spoke, she was remembering

Tom's words to her in that very room only two days before, 'I'm perfectly placed here. I hear everything . . .'

'I assure you he did.' Kemp's voice was very quiet.

'I won't believe you,' Elaine said, her voice trembling. 'I can't.' Turning from him, she groped her way towards the bed, blinded by her tears. 'Go away! Go now, or I shall call the servants.'

'And have your father find out the truth about Tom?' The words hung for a moment in the silence. He had come to stand only a few feet from her.

She froze. The threat was unmistakable. 'You would not tell Papa!' Overwhelmed with grief and fear, she was unable to hold back the tears any longer.

'As long as you do as I say, Tom's secret is safe.' His hands were on her shoulders, and he turned her unresistingly towards him. 'Defy me, and Tom's body will hang in chains till his bones turn to dust.'

She shrank from his hands, but he held her firmly. 'The shame would kill your father, Elaine.'

He saw fear, anger and defiance chase one another across her pale, tear-stained features and then the spark of fury that showed briefly in her amber eyes. For a long time they remained staring at each other, and she felt the shock of his determination like a blow. Defeated, she looked down, her long lashes veiling her expression.

'You are a cruel man, Master Kemp,' she whispered.

He gave a harsh laugh. 'Only when it is necessary. I am the soul of courtesy to those who give me their loyalty, I assure you.'

'And that is what you expect of me?' Her eyes blazed up at him again. 'Loyalty?'

He met her gaze levelly. 'I think I shall expect much more than loyalty from you,' he said after a pause. 'Much more.' Releasing her shoulders, he raised his hand almost absent-mindedly to brush a tear from her cheek with his fingertip.

Then he turned from her, looking down at the table beside her bed. There with the candle and a small vellum-bound Book of Hours lay the ruby necklace she had carelessly tossed aside only an hour or two earlier—a heap of sparkling stones the colour of fire. Picking them up thoughtfully, he weighed them in his hand.

She gave a bitter little laugh. 'Oh yes, they're valuable! They're worth a king's ransom, I believe. Take them, Master Kemp. Theft is your proud trade, after all, is it not? Why not take all my jewels? They lie there, in the casket. It is not even locked . . .'

She broke off with an exclamation of fear at the expression which crossed his face as he turned back to her. Throwing down the necklace, he seized her wrist and dragged her hard against him. She could feel the steel muscles of his chest, and then his hand was forcing her to look up at him. To her amazement, he was smiling. 'A spitfire indeed! No, my pretty, I shall leave you your king's ransom. The prize I seek is of far greater value. And I'm not so sunk in villainy that I would take a bauble like this from a child.' He released her and scooped the necklace into his palm once more. He smiled enigmatically. 'It would please me, however, to see it properly. Put it on.'

'No!' She stepped away from him hurriedly as he held out his hand. 'Why should you wish to see that? Leave me alone.'

'Put it on.' His tone had not changed, but there was determination in his eyes. They were hard as sapphires in the candlelight.

'I will not,' she whispered.

'Then I must do it for you.' He advanced and caught her wrist again, backing her against the high bed so that she had either to stop and submit to him or to fall back. Her heart beat frantically as she stood still, her head held proudly high while he reached up and fastened the necklace, lifting her hair carefully out of the way. Elaine held her breath as the strong square-tipped fingers gently stroked the stones. Then his hand was moving downwards, lightly touching the soft swell of her breast beneath her shift.

Acting so swiftly she did not know she had done it, she broke away from him, and struck him across the face as hard as she could. Then she ran for the door to the ante-room.

'Mab!' she screamed. 'Mab!'

But he was behind her; before she could utter another sound, his palm was clamped across her lips. She tasted bitter salt briefly as he lifted her off her feet, then he threw her face down on the bed.

'Another sound, sweetheart, and Tom's sister or no, I'll slit your tongue,' he breathed. 'Do you hear?' Without waiting for a sign that she had understood, he pulled her over to face him. There was a tight knot of panic in her stomach, but she could not fight him. She lay still, held by the warm light of his eyes, feeling his strength and his will as a tangible web that bound her.

He inclined his face slowly, and she submitted without a murmur as his lips claimed hers in a powerful kiss which left her trembling, every nerve quivering. He stared at her, the blue of his eyes deepening. 'So,' he said in a husky whisper. 'You do not find a pirate's kiss altogether distasteful.' He ran his finger lightly across her lips. Then, tracing a path down her throat, his hand moved towards the rubies, then on, light as a feather, towards the neckline of her shift, where he slipped his hand gently under the fine lawn to cup her breast. A pulse pounded in her throat. Every instinct told her to struggle and scream, yet still she could not move, held by his eyes as once more he lowered his lips to hers, his tongue probing gently till her mouth opened obediently beneath his, and she returned his kiss.

Abruptly he stopped, and sat up. The warmth faded from his eyes as she stared blindly at him, scarcely knowing what was happening to her.

In his face now was only the calculating hardness she had seen before. It brought a fresh stab of terror to her heart. He smiled coldly. 'I think we begin to understand each other, Tom's sister.' Pushing himself from the bed, he stood and looked down at her. 'Silence is all I ask of you for now. Tomorrow two of my men will bring your brother home. Tell your father whatever story you please, but remember,' he paused significantly, 'Tom's secret is in your hands.' He strode across the room and opened the door, then turned. 'I shall return soon. When I do, I shall expect your help.' He allowed himself a brief cynical smile.

'I trust you will be ready to give it wholeheartedly.'

Closing the door softly behind him, he disappeared into the darkness beyond.

For a moment, Elaine did not move. Then she turned over on the bed, and burying her head in the pillow, began to sob as though her heart would break. But not for long. In sudden terror that he might come back, she dragged herself up and ran over to the door, fumbling desperately with the key.

Then, slowly, she crossed to the window, and dashing the tears from her eyes, she stared out. The gardens were still deserted. Somewhere a barn owl screeched sharply, and she saw the pale shape of it drift by level with the window. Below, she heard the grating sound of the door being eased open in the ivy-covered wall, and Kemp emerged cautiously into the moonlight, his hand on the hilt of his cutlass. For a moment he stood to check, then he turned and looked up at her window. She drew back quickly, but he had seen her. He bowed low in her direction, sweeping the air with his free hand in a mocking salute, then sprinted towards the corner of the house.

Behind him, a shout echoed from the bushes near the wall. She saw Kemp whirl round, his cutlass in his hand. He stood still, staring into the darkness, before he ran towards the trees and was out of sight. After an instant, Sir Edward Brandon, the starlight glinting on the naked blade in his hand, burst out of the cover of the yew hedge and plunged after him in pursuit.

# CHAPTER
FOUR

ELAINE GASPED, shrinking back from the window. If Sir Edward caught him, Kemp would betray Tom. Of that she had no doubt at all. The man was completely unscrupulous, and he had no reason to want to preserve the Howard name. No reason except one: to force her to help him with his evil plans. 'Tom,' she whispered out loud in anguish. 'Oh, Tom!' Hot tears welled up in her eyes once more, and falling on her knees beside the bed, she cried until she could cry no more.

It was a long time before she dragged herself to her feet, aching with misery. The last feeble flickers of candle-light had burned themselves out, and she was shivering violently.

'Mab!' she called. She wanted suddenly to have the reassurance of a fire in the empty hearth, the comfort of another person to hold her in her arms. 'Mab, where are you?' Her voice broke into a sob.

She ran to the door which led into the small ante-chamber. Mab's truckle bed was empty, as she had known in her heart it must be. Retreating, she latched the door of her own room miserably and made her way back to the window. The garden was completely silent. There was nothing to tell her whether Kemp had made good his escape.

All she could do was to creep back into her bed. She pulled the covers over her and huddled in one corner, staring at the window as the dawn began to dim the stars; somewhere above the meadow beyond the yew walk the first lark began to sing.

It was broad daylight when she awoke, cramped and stiff. Mab was on her knees, folding clean linen into a chest in the corner, humming quietly to herself. Elaine raised herself on her elbow and tried to call out, but no sound came. Frightened, she wondered if she were dreaming, if the whole terrible night had been a dream.

'Mab?' she tried again. The call came out as a whisper, but the girl heard her.

'Mistress? Oh my Lord, child, your face!' Scrambling to her feet, Mab ran to the bed and took Elaine into her arms. 'What in the world have you been doing, my duck, your face is that swollen!'

'Where were you, Mab? Where were you when I needed you?' Elaine put her hands on the girl's shoulders and shook her gently.

Mab went white. 'I was asleep . . .' she stammered.

'You weren't there!' Elaine repeated, almost hysterically. 'You weren't there when I called!'

Mab blushed crimson, and looked down at her hands. 'It was after you'd gone out. I thought there'd be no harm . . .' she faltered. 'I went out to see my young man; I didn't think it was wrong if you were doing it, too.' She looked stubborn suddenly.

'If I were doing it, too . . . Oh, dear God!' Elaine pressed her hands to her face, feeling the tears well up once more.

'What is it?' Mab held her close. 'Aren't you well? Come, sit down again and tell me.'

'It's Tom!' Elaine cried almost hysterically. 'Tom is dead.'

'Dead?' Hastily Mab crossed herself. 'That can't be!'

'It can be.' Elaine stared at her wretchedly. 'And I have to tell Papa.'

While her maid was downstairs fetching a restorative drink, Elaine went over to her mirror. As Mab had said, her eyes were red and swollen from weeping. And there was a small cut on her lip. The sight of it brought a vivid tide of colour to her cheeks. She pressed her fingers to her mouth in anger and shame as she thought of Guy Kemp and his importunate kisses, his insolence and his threats. The ruby necklace was still clasped round her throat, a gaudy reminder of her visitor in the night. Her hands shaking with humiliation and fury, she unfastened it, throwing it down on the table as if the stones had burned her.

If anyone came to inquire where she was that morning, Mab must have sent them away, for she was not disturbed. It was late before she heard the horses of her father's guest being brought out and round to the front of the house, but only when the last hoofbeat had died away did she begin to dress, knowing that she could put off the hour no longer.

The house was completely silent, as though it knew already of the tragedy that had hit the family, as she made her way through the empty rooms and down the broad staircase. Her father would be, she knew, in his library. Taking a deep breath, she opened the door and went in, giving herself no time to think.

'Papa, there is something I must tell you.' Looking up, her eyes swimming with tears, she realised too late that he was not alone. Sir Edward lay sprawled in a chair by the window, a ledger open across his knees. Both men rose as they saw her, their faces registering concern.

Sir Edward reached her first. 'Mistress Elaine! What is it?' His hands outstretched for hers, his brown eyes full of anxiety, but she brushed past him, their previous night's unpleasant encounter almost forgotten as she threw herself into her father's waiting arms.

'It's Tom, Papa. Tom!' she cried in anguish, her carefully prepared words of gentleness and sympathy flying out of her head as her father's embrace encirled her. 'There's been an accident. He's dead!'

Her father stared down at her for a long moment, his face blank with shock. Before her eyes he appeared to crumple, his face becoming that of an old, old man as his arms fell away from her.

Quietly Sir Edward moved to his side, and Robert Howard clutched at his arm. But only for a moment. He straightened almost at once, and raised his chin with a determination she had not realised he possessed.

'Pour me a goblet of wine, there's a good fellow,' he murmured to Sir Edward as he groped behind him for a chair. He collapsed on to it, his face grey with fatigue. Quietly Sir Edward moved away to fill one of the silver cups standing on the sideboard, and returned to give it to his host. Then he filled another, and brought it to Elaine.

'May I suggest you sit down too,' he said gently. 'And drink this. It will give you strength.'

She took the goblet from him automatically, not even noticing the light touch of his fingers on hers as he pressed it into her hand.

'How did you hear about Tom?' She was conscious suddenly that Sir Edward was staring at her, and she looked at the floor. 'One of his servants came to me this morning.'

'Early this morning?' His eyes had become hard and probing. 'When your father's servants tried to reach you this morning, they were not admitted to your room.'

Too late, she saw the trap. She looked away from him defiantly, her fingers clutched white around the cold metal of the goblet. 'It must have been very early,' she said softly. 'Before dawn, I suppose. I don't remember clearly. Afterwards I told my maid to let no one in. I was too upset. I could not face Papa . . .' Tears poured down her cheeks. 'I loved my brother, sir,' she cried wildly. 'Why question me like this? All I know is that he is dead!'

He bowed slightly. 'And I am deeply grieved at your loss,' he said. But there was still suspicion in his voice.

They brought Tom's body home on a litter just before midday. He was escorted by four men, all soberly dressed. One of them, Elaine recognised with a sharp pang of fear, was the pirate who had accosted her at Kingston Point. He bowed to her gravely, as she stood looking down with frozen stillness at the pall, and drew her a little to one side.

'I thought you would want to know, mistress, that I gave him your message,' he said quietly. 'He knew that you had regretted your quarrel, and that you loved him and wished him well.'

She stared at him for a moment, then tears blinded her eyes and she fell to her knees beside the figure beneath the scarlet embroidered cloth.

Tom's body lay in state in the old church across the garden from the house, surrounded by incense and candles in the soft light of the medieval stained glass. After the

requiem, he was laid to rest with his mother and his
brothers and sisters in the Howard vault beneath the
church, while the two remaining members of his family
tried desperately to come to terms with life without him.
Slowly the pattern of life resumed. The pile of silken palls,
gifts from Tom's mourners, were folded away in the church,
the sprigs of rosemary lying on his tomb dried and
crumbled, and Elaine, dressed in a black gown and kirtle,
and sombre hood, went about her duties as before.

Sir Edward had never again mentioned the visitor in the
midnight garden, and if he pursued his enquiries about the
pirates on his daily rides to the quay and the warehouses
at Woodbridge, he did not speak of them in her presence.
And if she remembered Guy Kemp at all, it was firmly to
put any memories of him aside, shamefully conscious that
even the thought of the man and the hands that had roamed
so freely over her body for those few moments brought a
feeling of disquiet which had nothing to do with the terrible
news he had brought.

It was Mab who told her that *Black Witch* had gone.
They were in the still-room, making rose-water, when
she glanced shyly at Elaine, checking nervously over her
shoulder that they were alone. Then she reached into her
apron and produced a sealed letter.

'This is for you, mistress. I was given it in Woodbridge
and told to pass it to you in secret.'

All unsuspecting, Elaine took the letter and examined
the seal. It bore the imprint of a flying gull. She broke
it open and studied the scrawled message inside. Mab,
watching with interest, saw her face grow pale as death as
she read. Then, angrily, Elaine crumpled the letter up and
threw it into the still-room fire. 'Some stupid joke,' she
said, shrugging, as Mab stared at her, and she ran from
the room.

Elaine pressed her hands to her burning cheeks, trying
to calm herself as she ran through the house towards the
great staircase. The letter had been from Kemp. The
memory of his threats and his insolence, which had faded
to nothing compared with her grief for Tom, now returned
in full. She could see his tall figure as though it stood before

her, with his savage blue eyes and his arrogant strength, and she remembered that, but for him, Tom would still be alive!

She stopped by the virginal in the great hall and ran her finger violently over the keys. 'No, Master Kemp,' she breathed. 'I shall not remember our pact when you return to Woodbridge. I shall never help you!'

'Mistress Elaine?' The strong masculine voice behind her made her jump. 'I'm sorry. I didn't mean to startle you, but I thought you addressed me.' Sir Edward Brandon was looking at her from the far side of the room, an expression of cruel amusement crossing his face as the colour rose and faded in her cheeks. 'I have just come from your father's room. He wishes to speak to you.' He smiled, and she was aware suddenly of a new light in his eyes as he looked at her—a new confidence, and possibly something more.

Puzzled, she stared at him for a moment. Then she forced herself to return his smile, putting Guy Kemp for the moment to the back of her mind.

'I shall go to him at once,' she said, as graciously as she could. For the past weeks she had had no cause to complain of Sir Edward's manner, and her dislike of him had lessened now that she no longer feared for Tom. Nevertheless, as she let herself out of the door, she saw him watching her with a look of open triumphant glee.

Robert Howard was pottering about his library, but looked up as Elaine came in, and she noticed again how frail he had become since Tom's death. She kissed him warmly, however, and squeezed his arm.

'Not reorganising your library again, Papa?'

He shook her off gently. 'Why not, pray? It's one of the few things I can do which I enjoy, and which doesn't exhaust me.' He coughed fretfully. 'Now, girl, sit down, sit down. I want to talk to you, and I am too tired to argue, do you understand?'

He sat down heavily on the oak settle, and she saw with alarm that he was pressing his hand to his side as though in pain.

'Papa!'

'No, girl, sit down.' He shook her off testily and, chastened, she obeyed him, gathering her skirts round her and sinking on to a stool at his feet.

He looked down at her thoughtfully, and at last she saw his tired face break into a smile. 'Sweet child, I wonder, has it crossed your mind that, since your brother's death, you have become my only heir?' She saw the wave of unhappiness cross his face at the mention of Tom, but in a second it had passed and he was resolute once more. 'You will one day inherit my houses and farms, my ships, my business, my wealth—everything.'

Elaine swallowed. 'But, Papa, you may yet marry again. You're quite young; you could have other sons . . .' Her heart cried out against the thought of there ever being someone else to take Tom's place, but her father's unhappiness was more than she could bear.

He shook his head. 'No, child. It is too late. There will be no more sons.' He reached out and touched her cheek. 'I have been pondering about how to ensure that your inheritance is safeguarded. There will scarcely be a man in the kingdom who will not wish to marry you, and I may have very little time to see that you are safely disposed of.'

Elaine stared up at his face, full of a sudden terrible misgiving, 'Papa?'

'No, child. Be silent. We have discussed your marriage on numerous occasions'—he gave a rueful smile—'and always you have talked me out of any alliance I might have considered. But I had to reach a decision. And it is made.' Stiffly he stood up and walked to the window. Elaine stared after him, numb with apprehension. For a moment she could not speak as the silence stretched out between them. At last he turned.

'I have agreed to your betrothal to Sir Edward Brandon.'

'No!' With a cry, she caught at her father's hand. 'No, Papa! I will not marry him!'

His eyes were full of sorrow as he gently disengaged his hand. 'I have already signed the preliminary agreements with him,' he said softly. 'My mind is made up.'

'I won't marry him, Papa. You cannot make me!' Scarcely knowing what she did, Elaine slipped to her knees at her father's feet. 'Please, Papa! You cannot insist!'

'Sit down here, child.' He pulled her down beside him on the settle. His face had paled to the colour of old parchment and his breath was coming in harsh gasps.

'Edward is a fine young man—and he is handsome, which I believe counts much with you ladies.' He attempted a smile. 'He knows much of my business already and has handled it with skill these past weeks since Tom's death. I trust him, Elaine. And I trust very few men.' He looked at her pleadingly. 'He also has another great recommendation, one which I confess I did not know before. It helped me finally to make up my mind when he asked me for your hand. You know it has always grieved me that, for all our wealth, our family has never been ennobled. True, we are distantly connected to the Norfolk Howards, but I had wished one day to please the King enough to win a title of my own.' He sighed. 'It is too late for me, Elaine, but Sir Edward is related to the Duke of Suffolk and, more important still, will be successor to his cousin the Earl of Thetford, who has no wife.' There was a feverish sparkle in his eyes as he scanned her face.

Elaine was pale as milk. 'And that won you to his cause, Papa?' she said through dry lips.

He nodded. 'That convinced me. My property will be secure, and my daughter will be a countess and welcomed at court. I shall be able to die in peace.' He broke into a paroxysm of coughing.

She stared at him in sudden terror as he gasped and spluttered, then jumped up and ran for the wine. 'Papa, don't . . . Please don't be upset. You're not going to die yet. Not for years, Papa!' With a shaking hand she held the cup to his lips. But after a sip or two he calmed a little, and a smudge of colour returned to his face.

'Obey me quietly in this, Elaine,' he breathed. 'I have no wish to force you, but force you I will if I have to.' His voice was gaining in strength. 'And I may not live long. I half have it in mind that I would rather be with your mother and Tom now, in the church.' He sighed. 'Do I have your promise that you will obey me?'

For a moment she could not answer. The room spun and

rocked until she thought she was going to faint, then it steadied, and she saw her father's taut, anxious face and she knew she could not do anything to put his health any more at risk. She forced herself to give a little smile.

'You have my promise, Papa.'

Sir Edward was waiting for her in the great hall. She shrank back with dislike as she saw him, but already he was coming towards her, a thin smile on his lips.

'I can see by the look on your face that your father has told you of our agreement. I hope it is not too displeasing to you?' He caught her hands and drew her to him.

She tried to pull away. 'I am afraid you must give me some time to grow used to the idea, Sir Edward,' she said coldly. She struggled to free herself, but in a moment he had an arm round her waist, pulling her hard against him.

'Such maidenly modesty is hardly necessary,' he whispered harshly, as his lips sought hers. 'You need not pretend with me, sweetheart. I am a man of the world.'

'Pretend?' Struggling harder now, Elaine tried to tear her wrists free. 'Please let me go . . .' But her words were stifled as his mouth claimed hers with triumphant possession. Closing her mind as best she could, she froze, submitting to his embraces with stony immobility. Almost at once he released her, as if his desire had gone once she stopped fighting him.

'That's better, though hardly the warm greeting I would expect from my betrothed,' he said unpleasantly. 'Don't tell me your indifference means that you had hoped to marry your pirate lover!'

'What do you mean?' Her heart was hammering furiously as she looked at the gloating face of the man who stood before her.

He smiled coldly. 'I mean the man whom you wave to on the deck of a caravel that slips out of Woodbridge in the night; I mean the man you visit in a bawdy tavern where no lady should be seen; I mean the man who creeps up to your bed by way of a secret stair in the moonlight.' His voice had sunk to a whisper as he shot out his hand and seized her arm once again. 'Oh, do not fear, my Elaine!

I shall not tell your doting father that the daughter he offers me is not a virgin. I shall not tell him she consorts with the very men who rob him. That would break his heart, would it not?' He pulled her close until her face was only inches from his. 'I can keep silent, my dear . . . if I want to.' He released her so suddenly that she staggered. 'I will not even ask you—yet—the name of your lover.' He smiled thoughtfully. 'Once we are married and your allegiance is totally mine, then I shall make you tell me everything about him. Or, perhaps, by then I shall have taken him, and you shall watch me put him to the question at my leisure before I hang him.'

Elaine flinched, afraid that she was going to faint. 'You're wrong,' she cried. 'You are quite wrong! I have no lover, and I have never consorted with the pirates.'

'No?' His eyes were like gimlets. 'Then who was it you waved to with such emotion on the deck of that ship? Who was it who saluted you at your window? A stranger, perhaps? Your dead brother's servant?'

Her retort froze on her lips. 'Yes.' She grasped at the lead he had unwittingly given her. 'At my window it was Tom's servant.' Her voice faded away, as his eyes held hers, mocking. She was remembering the night Guy Kemp came to her room, and the way he had comforted her after he had given her the news. How strange that, overwhelmed by her memories of his insolence and his threats, she had forgotten that one sweet moment of tenderness.

Edward seemed to be trying to read her mind. An unpleasant sneer curled his lip. 'No matter, sweetheart, who it was. I'll have little time for you, virgin or not, you'll be glad to hear. I have a lady at home who keeps me more than satisfied.' He laughed at the blush which mantled her cheeks. 'She'll not be pleased to see you. I suspect she'll flay me alive when I take you back to Aldebourne. But when she hears of the wealth you bring with you, she may change her mind.' He laughed again.

'Do you so blatantly covet my money, Sir Edward?' Elaine was shivering, in spite of the warmth of the afternoon.

'Why not? Your father understands. Our agreement is

clear. Your wealth, for the title I shall one day inherit. A
bargain, don't you think? But don't fret. I'll have some
time for you; enough to ensure that you are an obedient
and fruitful wife.' He raised her face to look at it with
insolent attention. 'Oh yes, Elaine, I shall have a little time
for you. But now I have other things to do, if you will
excuse me.' He bowed.

She watched him walk the length of the room and disappear through the door before she sank on the nearest chair,
her heart pounding with anger and fear.

Time and time again over the next few days Elaine
pleaded with her father to release her from her promise
before the formal betrothal was made, but he would not
listen. Deaf to her pleas and her tears, he called his lawyers
to meet Sir Edward to talk of jointures and portions and
estates and farms, and the final binding betrothal was
made, and the date of the wedding fixed. It was to be
Midsummer Day.

Robert Howard's two unmarried sisters descended on
the house with a retinue of maids and dressmakers, and
Elaine was forced to endure hours of fittings as her wedding
gowns were made. Room after room vanished beneath
clouds of silks and damasks, velvets and brocades, and
Mab grew almost hysterical with excitement as she ordered
the visiting servants about and gloried in her position as
Elaine's personal maid.

Amid all the noise, Elaine herself grew more silent. A
cold chain of misery seemed to be bound about her heart
as she moved in a dream, trailing from room to room at
her aunts' beck and call. To her relief she scarcely saw Sir
Edward at all, and when she did, there was no sign of the
savage triumph he had displayed the day their marriage
had been agreed. It was as if now that he was sure of her,
he had lost interest in her. For several days he disappeared,
riding to his great house at Aldebourne to warn his servants
there to make ready for a new mistress, and Elaine
breathed again. But then he returned, attended by several
young men and servants, and as he bowed and kissed her
hand in greeting, she saw again the cruelty which lurked
in his eyes.

Each night she would dutifully sip the possets that Mab produced for her, then sink into her bed and lie awake, as the hours slipped by, trying to force her mind to merciful blankness. When sleep eventually came, it was the deep blackness of total exhaustion.

Two weeks before her wedding, Kemp reappeared. He was waiting for her with three of his men as she rode back across the heath with Mab after visiting her godmother's house at Bromeswell. They were walking their horses slowly over the rabbit-cropped turf, several paces ahead of the two escorting grooms, when without warning the four men rose from the undergrowth.

Mab gave a little scream, but it was bitten off short as she found herself staring at the glinting blade of a dagger. In a moment, she and the two grooms had been led away and Elaine was alone, looking down into Kemp's face as he took a firm hold of her horse's bridle. Her fear was followed by a sharp sense of shock as she realised that it was the first time she had seen him clearly in daylight. His teeth were brilliant white in his deeply tanned face as he sketched a low bow. 'Mistress Elaine, I trust you have not forgotten our tryst.' His eyes were the colour of the sky arching high above.

She swallowed nervously, her gloved hands clutching at the scarlet reins. 'I could not believe you meant it, Master Kemp,' she managed to retort.

The heath was deserted. A shimmering heat-haze hung over the low bushes, and the silence was broken only by the clink of the horse's bridle as it shook its head, annoyed by the weight of the man's hand on its bit. The air was full of the bitter-sweet scent of gorse.

'You could not believe I meant it?' he repeated. 'Then I must convince you, it seems.' His tone was pleasant, but she heard the slight hint of a threat behind it and shivered in spite of the warmth of the afternoon.

She stared down at him. He was tall, as she had found out that night in her bedroom, and broad shouldered, and the salt-stained leather jerkin did little to hide his muscular physique. In his belt, besides the vicious cutlass, was a small carved dagger. There was something violent and frightening about him, but at the same time something alarmingly attractive, and suddenly, in spite of her fear and anger, she saw what it was that must have drawn Tom to this man's side and made him his friend, and what it was that had made her respond so wantonly to his kisses, whilst those of her betrothed left her cold and afraid. The compelling charm of the man was reaching out to her once more now, and she could not help reacting automatically with a quickening of the breath and a little nervous smile.

'How did you know I would be riding here?' she asked after a moment.

His eyes narrowed a little. 'I have my spies.'

'And what makes you think that my servants will remain quiet about our meeting?'

He grinned. 'That will be for you to ensure! I know you will find a way of persuading them that it would be in your father's best interests not to alarm him unduly.'

She bit her lip in quick anger. 'You seem to have outmanoeuvred me, sir. And what is it that you wish to say to me, now that you have so cleverly managed to arrange our tryst, as you call it?' She tried to hide her nervousness by patting the horse's neck.

'The time has come for you to help me,' he said swiftly, lowering his voice. 'There are two things you must find out; then tomorrow evening you must be prepared to come aboard *Black Witch*. You will be away for three days at most if the wind holds. Bring as little as you can. A small coffer is all I allow. And you will come alone.'

She gasped in disbelief. 'I cannot come with you!'

'You must.' His hand came down on both of hers, pressing them against the high pommel of the saddle. 'Nothing I ask of you is too hard, Elaine. I wish to know the date your father expects to receive his shipments. And I want you to bring with you your father's seal of authority. Do you understand?'

'No!' Her eyes were suddenly blazing with anger. Pulling her hands free of his, she raised her whip. 'Let go of my horse, sir! I shall have nothing to do with your plans. Nothing!'

Desperately trying to wrench the mare's head from his grasp, she kicked the black flanks, lashing at Kemp's head and hands. Cressid leaped forward and reared with a whistling scream of panic, but in a second Kemp's hand had closed over Elaine's, twisting the whip out of her grasp before he pulled her headlong from the saddle. She fell heavily on the sandy ground, and lay, too stunned to move or speak. Behind her, she was conscious that he had retained his hold on the horse to calm it, and was tethering it to a fallen tree. Only then did he turn his attention back to her.

'I trust you are not hurt,' he said curtly as he pulled her to her feet.

Speechless with anger, she shrank away from him.

'How dare you lay hands on me?' she cried. 'My father will have you flogged when he catches up with you.'

He smiled at her, his blue eyes dancing suddenly. 'Me? Flogged? I think not, mistress.' Then the humour had gone as swiftly as it had come. 'He would not flog Tom's partner in crime, his son's dearest friend, would he? I think you forget that it was Tom's last wish that you hide his connection with me from your father.'

Elaine glared at him unhappily. Was there any way in which she could fight this man, knowing he would always be able to defeat her by cynically manipulating her love for her father? Trembling, she turned from him, and realised nervously that her horse's sudden terrified cavorting had carried them out of sight of the others. She and Guy Kemp were alone.

She swallowed hard, trying to recover some vestige of courage. 'You know I will do anything to save Papa from that knowledge,' she said at last.

'Then you will do as I ask. A date, a seal, and three days from your life. That is all I ask, mistress,' he said, more gently this time. 'You won't find me constantly returning to demand your help. This one piece of business in Tom's memory, and then you will never see me again.'

She turned to face him, 'There is something you should

know: why I cannot go with you tomorrow, even if I wished it.' She looked up at him wearily. 'I am to marry Sir Edward Brandon on Midsummer Day.'

A conflict of emotions played over his face, and his eyes darkened enigmatically. 'Are you, indeed? The man who dares to think he can capture *Black Witch* by spreading his gold and his spies around the taverns and ale houses.' He laughed bitterly. 'So, he has been wooing my little Elaine as well.' He face became harsh. 'And does it please you, this marriage?' His eyes held hers, and she could feel the colour mounting in her cheeks.

'It pleases me very much,' she managed to retort. 'As it will when he catches you and hangs you.'

He frowned. 'So, you intend to confide in him, do you, this new husband of yours? You'll tell him of your pirate friend, and beg him to keep your secret while he hunts me down? You have already told him about Tom's activities, of course . . .'

'Well, no . . .' She hung her head. 'I couldn't tell him about Tom . . .'

His eyes narrowed. 'But I would, sweetheart. One thing you should know. When they bring a man of my calling to trial, they torture him first, to make him tell the names of his colleagues. I'm a brave man, I think, but I doubt if under torture even I would shield a dead man's name.'

She stared at him, aghast. 'Torture?' she whispered through stiff lips.

'Of course. King Henry wishes to discourage piracy, as he does other crime. In particular, successful crime.'

'And you are, of course, successful?' She managed a small smile.

He bowed. 'And intend to remain so. With your help.'

She shook her head slowly. 'I can't help you.'

'You can, Elaine. You have no choice, unless you want your father's illusions destroyed. Tomorrow evening my lieutenant will come for you. You may tell your father that you are staying with Mistress Ashley, your godmother, for three days, while she instructs you in some basic wifely skills.' Again the flash of humour showed in his eyes. 'She and I are old friends, and she will not give you away.'

'I don't believe you,' Elaine whispered. 'Aunt Margaret would never be a friend to someone like you!'

He grinned. 'You will have to ask her that yourself, sometime. It would surprise you, I think, to learn the names of some of my friends. Now, before Sam Fletcher comes for you tomorrow, make sure you have the seal. Your father will understand, I am sure, that in your nervous state you picked it up and dropped it into your pocket by mistake. Your maid will accompany you as far as Bromeswell. Then she will stay with Mistress Ashley out of sight until you return.'

'Why can't she come with me?' There was something like panic in Elaine's voice.

'Because one woman on a ship is like to prove an encumbrance,' he replied brutally. 'Two would be a disaster. And make sure she knows how to hold her tongue, for your father's sake.'

He fell silent, looking down at her. Then, as though only half realising what he did, he raised his hand to touch the lock of hair that had escaped her headdress and was curling loose on her shoulder. 'I hope you know what you are doing, Tom's sister, marrying Ned Brandon.'

Her eyes widened, and she felt the colour rising to her cheeks once more. 'You speak as though you know him.'

He grinned bitterly. 'I do indeed. We were neighbours once, he and I. I think it would please him immensely if he were to learn the name of the man he is trying to hang.'

'You were enemies then?'

He laughed. 'My brother and he were friends, put it that way. But my story is not one I tell, even to you, sweetheart. Come, you did not answer my question. Do you know what you are about, marrying him?'

'It is arranged. My father is satisfied, and I do not find Sir Edward unattractive.' It seemed very important somehow that he should not guess how much she had come to hate her betrothed.

'But do you love him?' His eyes held hers.

'I like him very much, Master Kemp. More than I have ever liked anyone else,' she replied with spirit. 'But I fail to see that how I feel is any business of yours.'

She started towards her horse. 'I will help you tomorrow because it seems that I must. But beyond that, I see no reason for us to speak again. If you will move out of my way, I shall go to find my servants.'

He did not stir. Hands on hips he grinned down at her, effectively barring the path. 'It would be churlish to leave without saying goodbye, mistress,' he said.

'I feel churlish, sir! Do you think my brother would have allowed you to be so familiar with me if he were here?'

'I think the answer to that would surprise you, Elaine,' he said softly. 'He spoke of you often and with much affection, and he told me of the processions of eager suitors you had turned away and the need one day for you to be furnished with a husband who would be capable of ruling you.' He paused thoughtfully. 'I only regret that the one you have chosen is Ned Brandon. However, chosen him you have, and it will give me enormous pleasure to know I have stolen a further kiss from his bride!'

His strong arms had enfolded her before she knew what he was about, and his lips, seeking hers, were demanding and powerful. She started to pull away, but then, hardly realising that they did so, her lips parted eagerly beneath his kisses, and she stood helpless in his embrace, feeling a delicious languor creep over her limbs. The hot sky spun into a dome of gold as her arms slipped treacherously about his neck.

It was a long time before he released her and looked down at her, his eyes enigmatic. 'I look forward to our next meeting, mistress. It promises well,' he said softly.

She was horrified, her cheeks burning with shame, but already he had turned away. Stooping, he released the rein of her horse, and almost before she knew it, his hands were on her slim waist and she was in the saddle.

'Until tomorrow, Tom's sister,' he said with a chuckle, and sweeping his cap from his head, sketched an elaborate bow. Then he turned, and with a shrill whistle to his henchmen, he vanished into the tangle of gorse and brambles.

# CHAPTER
# FIVE

MOMENTS LATER, Mab and the two servants appeared, leading their horses at the run. At the sight of her mistress, Mab burst into tears. 'Oh my love, I thought you'd been killed!'

Shakily Elaine steadied Cressid. She was frantically trying to think of something to say to the three anxious people which would reassure them and at the same time ensure that they understood her need for complete secrecy. Then her problem was abruptly solved for her. The elder of her two escorts, John Palmer, who had been her brother's man, smiled knowingly, his eyes gleaming in the sunlight.

'We'll tell no one of this incident, Mistress Elaine. I know he was Master Tom's friend,' he said quietly.

'You know?' she echoed in disbelief. She had not seen any sign of recognition pass between the two men.

He nodded. 'Will and Mabbet will stay silent, too, if that is your wish, you may depend on it.' He was watching her face closely.

'Yes.' She was still trying to compose herself. 'Yes, that is my wish. No one must know that we met him here.' She could feel herself becoming agitated again, in spite of his reassuring manner.

'No one will ever find out from us.' He snapped his fingers at Mab and Will. 'Mount up,' he commanded. 'We are late, and Mistress Elaine must not be missed.' Releasing her bridle, he swung himself on to his own horse and fell in next to her on the track which led towards home.

For the rest of the ride, Elaine retreated into her own anxieties, trying to think of a way to accomplish the tasks Guy Kemp had set her, and long after she was once more

at King's Brook she had still not been able to see her father
alone. Sir Edward had been at his side the whole time since
his return from his estates, and this day seemed to be no
exception. Tired and depressed, she retired to her room.

Her father had two seals. A large official one, which was
carried by one of his clerks in a leather pouch, and a smaller
signet which he wore on the forefinger of his left hand.
Both were as inaccessible as a piece of the rainbow.

Increasingly panic-stricken, she went down to supper,
only to find that one of her problems was being solved for
her. The men were discussing the very shipment that Kemp
had asked her about, talking with easy familiarity across
the top of her head as if she were not there at all. Her
father could not conceal his excitement.

'The ships have been delayed for months by storms and
sickness on their voyage back from Venice.' He reached
for his wine, colour showing in his cheeks. 'But they are
now on the last lap of their journey, and wait only for the
next fair wind to bring them home.'

'How many ships are there, Papa?' Elaine asked, her
eyes almost unwillingly straying to the signet on his finger.

Her father looked at her, surprised at this sudden interest
after her long rebellious silences at meals. Then he smiled
with a pleased shrug. 'Four galleons left Woodbridge. One
was mine, the others belonged to three other merchants.
*Star*, James Carpenter's ship, foundered, but the three
others return.' He rubbed his hands together.

Elaine noticed then that Sir Edward was watching her,
with his lip curled cynically.

'Why this curiosity I wonder, about the number of ships,'
he asked softly. 'Does it reflect your new-found interest in
the sea?'

She could feel herself colouring under his gaze, and
looked away quickly. 'I have no interest in the sea, Sir
Edward,' she retorted. 'Only in my father's welfare. What
interests him, interests me.'

'And you don't wish to know how the galleons are armed
or the numbers of their crew?' His eyes were merciless as
they bored into hers.

'I should very much like to know both, of course,' she

said defiantly. 'And every detail with which you can furnish me!'

Her anger, fuelled by the knowledge that, this time, she really was the spy he suspected her to be, exploded in her eyes, and for a moment he looked taken aback. Then he smiled.

'They are well armed, Elaine,' he said smoothly. 'More than well. They have fought pirates off Spain and Algiers and in the bay of Syracuse to bring their cargoes home, and their crews are unscathed.'

Behind her, her father shook his head sadly. 'No, my boy, you are wrong. They have been very unlucky. The letter my messenger brought from Antwerp says that the ships are sadly undermanned. Sickness has taken many of the men and many have deserted. Had they been attacked, they would have stood little chance.'

Elaine felt a little treacherous surge of triumph as she turned back to her betrothed and saw the anger on his face. She forced herself to laugh lightly. 'Had I been what you suspected, Sir Edward, I should have been glad to have that information,' she murmured, so that her father could not hear.

By the time she had bidden her father good night and returned to her room with Mab, she was still no nearer to thinking of a way to obtain her father's seal. The more she racked her brains to try to produce some plan, the more worried she became. Kemp's face kept appearing in her mind; with the implacable coldness of his eyes that replaced so swiftly the far-away look as he kissed her, and the cruel twist of his lips when he threatened to expose Tom, haunting her.

Long after she had gone to bed she lay awake, listening to Mab's steady breathing on the truckle bed in the corner. She had insisted that her maid sleep with her every night since Kemp's visit to her room, terrified that he might reappear although the door beneath the ivy was now securely bolted.

The thought of Kemp made Elaine blush violently, and her mind returned to their encounter on the heath. It did not seem possible that a man of such unscrupulous cruelty would also be the one who had with his insolent caresses turned her body to fire and melted her resentment and anger to helpless delight. She could not understand herself; her body had seemed to react quite independently of her feelings, and the realisation filled her with shame. She shuddered, and dragged her mind back to the seal, not allowing herself to remember even for an instant that one of the ships they had been discussing that evening belonged to her father. The anguish he would suffer at the loss of his cargo was still a thousand times less than anything that he would suffer if he were to find out about Tom. She was trapped, and she could do nothing but obey Kemp's instructions. And, to do that, she had to obtain the seal.

Only one course of action seemed possible. To creep down to the library now, while the household was asleep, and see if she could find it. She sat up reluctantly, half hoping that Mab would wake, but with a little snort and a mutter, Mab threw out her arm and turned over, then lay quietly again and her breathing steadied. Cautiously Elaine slid out of bed, wrapped her cloak round her and tiptoed towards the door. The heavy latch stuck briefly, and then came free with a rattle. She held her breath, but Mab did not stir again.

Trembling with anxiety, she let herself into the next bedroom. Her Aunt Mary was fast asleep, snoring in the high bed, the curtains tightly pulled. On a low bed in the corner a maid lay, mouth open in the faint moonlight. Leaving the door ajar, she tiptoed on through the successive bedrooms. No one heard her. Only in the great hall below did the dogs stir and raise their heads. Breathing more freely now, she thrust a taper into the embers of the fire to light a candle before she moved on towards her father's library. The faint circle of candlelight showed the big table covered with books and manuscripts, and a carved chair, also piled high—but no seal.

Beyond the library was a small room used by Robert Howard's clerks and transcribers as an office. She held the candle at arm's length and peered in. It was barely furnished with two stools, a shelf piled high with documents, the chequer table on which the clerks did their accounts, and the high desk with its ink-pots and quills, an abacus and rolls of unused parchment. And there, on the corner, lay the bag. Elaine caught it up, her heart beating as she prayed the seal would be there and not locked away. But her fingers found its hard shape at once and she extracted it carefully, then replaced the bag on the desk, glancing as she did so at the black, unshuttered windows, each pane of glass reflecting accusingly the bright flame of her candle. Shamed, she blew it out, and made her way back.

It seemed to her that she did not breathe again until she had regained her bedroom. She thrust the seal deep under her feather pillows and jumped into bed. In the corner, Mab had never stirred.

Next morning, while the maid was downstairs fetching her hot water, Elaine snatched the seal from the pillow. She had to leave it somewhere secure because there would certainly be an outcry as soon as its loss was discovered, and it was more than likely that her father would have the whole house searched. Fumbling in her haste, she found the key to her jewel chest in its usual hiding-place in the beam above her head. She unlocked it and threw back the lid. A pile of jewels sparkled up at her, on the top of them the ruby necklace, but the packet of letters Tom had given her had gone. She stared down at the casket in horror, then she emptied it on the bed. Silver and gold chains, an ivory rosary, enamelled brooches, pearls, rings and pendants spilled out, but no letters. She looked round the room, half expecting to see the packet lying on the table or on the floor, but there was no sign of it, and she knew that she had locked it away safely.

Putting everything back, she dropped the seal into the casket with the jewellery, locked it and looked at the small key in her hand. 'Was it you, Mab?' She turned furiously on the maid as she staggered in with a pitcher of fast-cooling water. 'Did you take Tom's letters?' The look of blank incomprehension on Mab's face answered the question for her before the girl could open her mouth.

With a shiver of fear, Elaine glanced back at the little chest as she went downstairs, the key safely knotted this time to the end of her long silk girdle. Until that morning she had barely given a thought to Tom's packet of letters and the mysterious Mistress Lockesley who would come to claim them, but now, without quite knowing why, the loss of the letters filled her with foreboding.

The expected uproar about the loss of the seal never came. Robert Howard, in a high good mood, had decided to dispatch his two clerks on an errand to Norwich as soon as they had broken their fast, and himself prepared to go down to Woodbridge with Sir Edward. The door of the little office behind the library remained closed.

Elaine watched her father leave with an overwhelming feeling of sadness. By the time he returned, she would have gone, and he would never know how much she was risking for his sake. She tried to close her mind to the thought of what the evening would bring, but the knowledge that she was trapped as surely as if Kemp held her under lock and key kept coming back to her. She had to go to her fate willingly and agree to anything he had arranged for her to do. The thought was not a pleasant one.

The day passed slowly, as she followed Aunt Mary and Aunt Jane through the hollow tasks of preparing for her wedding as the tension inside her built up and in the courtyard the shadow inexorably moved round the sundial. She asked Mab to pack them both small trunks with a change of clothes, telling her that they would be away for a few days with Mistress Ashley. In the end, it was almost with relief that she heard her whisper late in the afternoon. 'Mistress Elaine, the steward from your godmother's farm is here to escort us to Bromeswell.'

Elaine looked up from her stitching, her stomach knotting with fear. But she rose calmly, kissing each of her aunts on the cheek, explaining that a visit to Mistress Ashley had been arranged; then she made her way with every show of outward confidence towards her room.

The small trunks with a change of clothes were ready, and her cloak laid on the bed. Bidding the girl take the boxes down, Elaine waited for her to disappear, then, her fingers clumsy with haste, she unlocked the casket and retrieved her father's seal.

Two men were waiting with four horses openly on the carriageway in front of the house. She recognised neither of them as they bowed to her. Mab was already seated on one of the horses, the trunks strapped behind the men's saddles.

The elder introduced himself as Sam Fletcher, then he helped Elaine to mount. He was elegantly if soberly dressed, but the clothes could not disguise the deep rich tan of his skin which could have come only from the sea, or the serviceable sword and brace of daggers thrust into his belt.

Determined not to let him see her fear, Elaine sat proudly erect as she gathered her reins. Neither man had spoken as they set off up the drive, and the oppressive silence was somehow more frightening than any speech would have been. Even Mab had grown quiet, glancing in puzzlement at her mistress as they rode.

They rode towards Woodbridge along tracks, avoiding the roads until they reached the village of Melton, where they halted.

At last Fletcher spoke. He reached forward and took the rein of Mab's horse. 'Get up behind the lad there,' he commanded curtly. 'He'll take you to Mistress Ashley at Bromeswell.' He turned to Elaine. 'Have you told the girl to hold her tongue?' Elaine shook her head miserably. 'Then do so now. You know the risk if she doesn't.'

She looked at Mab pleadingly. 'You must go on to Mistress Ashley alone, Mab, and stay there until I return,' she said quietly. 'If anyone asks for me, you must say I am ill and can see no one.' She swallowed desperately. 'Please, Mab. Tell no one at all that I have gone.'

'You're going to him?' Mab said incredulously. 'To Kemp! He's your lover?'

Elaine gulped. 'No! He's not my lover.'

But Mab's face had blossomed into happy smiles. 'Oh, my love, I'll not tell a soul. They won't drag it out of me with wild horses!'

Elaine shuddered, glancing at the impassive face of her escort. But she knew it was sensible to let Mab go on thinking she was going to an assignation with her lover.

That was a secret the girl would know how to keep.

Then Mab was gone, jolting behind the younger man on the back of his horse, and Elaine and her guide were alone.

Almost at once he plunged back into the woods, leading the horse which carried her box at a brisk trot, gesturing her to follow. The track he took was almost imperceptible, winding steeply down towards the river through the fresh green bracken. They rode north, following the curving banks of the river where it narrowed dramatically to meander through soft meadows bordered with reed-beds. Only when they were across it did they turn eastward, splashing the horses through the sandy shallows, keeping up a steady fast pace.

'Where are we going?' Elaine could bear his silence no longer. She felt sick with fear, and tired after her sleepless night and the long day of tension.

Fletcher reined back slightly to ride beside her. 'Not far now. The *Witch* is anchored out in the tideway a bit further down the river.'

With a shudder, Elaine glanced beyond him to where the water was widening rapidly now as they rode towards the sea, the grey tide running in strongly. A cluster of boats were anchored in the centre of the water, their bows pointing towards the sea, but there was no sign of the raked masts of the caravel. The wind off the land carried the smell of pines and bracken. There was no hint in the air of the open sea half a dozen miles away. The sun was low now as it fell towards a bank of purple storm-cloud. The tide would soon be high.

They had been riding for some time in the deepening twilight when they rounded a corner and Elaine saw *Black Witch* anchored in the tideway, the three masts almost invisible against the dark trees of the opposite side of the hidden bay. She tightened her grip on the horse, resisting the urge to turn and gallop in the opposite direction. As if sensing her terror, her escort reined back beside her and reached across to take her bridle.

'We'll leave the horses here,' he said abruptly. 'A boy will come by and by to take them to the farm.'

Helping her to dismount, he untied her small trunk and